The Pet War

THE PET WAR

ALLAN WOODROW

SCHOLASTIC INC.

Copyright © 2013 by Allan Woodrow

This book was originally published in hardcover by Scholastic Press in 2013.

All rights reserved. Published by Scholastic Inc., *Publishers since 1920*. SCHOLASTIC and associated logos are trademarks and/or registered trademarks of Scholastic Inc.

ISBN 978-0-545-51320-3

12 11 10 9 8 7 6 5 4 3 2 1   15 16 17 18 19 20/0

Printed in the U.S.A.   40
This edition first printing 2015
Book design by Yaffa Jaskoll

TO MADELYN AND EMMY. AND EMMY AND MADELYN.

NOT NECESSARILY IN THAT ORDER.

CHapteR 1

I stood at the bottom of the driveway in my pajamas with a serious case of bed head. Across the street, a large yellow rental moving van backed out of our neighbor's driveway. I felt a cold, deep pang of loneliness seep through my body.

Or maybe it was just the wind. These weren't very warm pajamas.

From the driver's seat, Mr. Finch smiled at me. He stuck his hand out the window, his other hand on the steering wheel. "Bye, Otto," he said. "Take care!"

"I'll miss you!" I hollered. But I wasn't yelling to Mr. Finch. I wouldn't miss *him*. I screamed to Alfalfa, their golden retriever, who sat in the backseat. I think I even heard an *Arf!*, a single gruff, depressed bark answering my shout.

"Bye!" I croaked, my yell catching in my throat. I couldn't hear much over the loud clacking of the truck. But I imagined a bark rang out as full of sadness and misery as I felt.

Then they were gone — the Finches, Alfalfa, and their truckload of stuff — around the corner and out of sight. Mom said a new family would be moving into the house in a few weeks. I asked if they had a dog, or if they had kids, or if they were professional soccer players.

Mom said no, no, and she highly doubted it.

I stood in the driveway for a moment longer, lonely, shivering, and wishing I'd worn shoes.

I'd feared this day. I'd feared it for weeks. So I'd pretended it was never going to happen. But ignoring bad things never worked. I sometimes ignored my homework and watched TV. But then I just had to do my homework the next day and Mom wouldn't let me watch television for a week. Unfortunately, things don't vanish just because you stop paying attention to them. Too bad. If they did, I'd have just ignored my sister, Lexi — and *poof!* — life would have been perfect.

But I figured life was going to stink now that Alfalfa had left. I had played with him almost every day since he was a puppy. I mean, the dog was practically more mine than the Finches'. I knew which ear he liked scratched (the right ear), his favorite game (keep-away with the tennis ball), and exactly how long he wanted his tummy rubbed (until he barked twice).

Alfalfa's new neighbors, whoever they were, wouldn't know any of that. What if they didn't even like dogs? What if they liked *cats*?

There are two types of people in the world: dog people and cat people. Dog people are clever, friendly, good-looking, funny, and overall fantastically wonderful. Cat people, on the other hand, are ugly, boring, and smell bad. I'm not making that up — those are the facts.

I, by the way, am a dog person.

But now that Alfalfa had moved away, there was only one thing I could do. Well, there were two things I could do. The first thing was to move to Montana into the house next door to the Finches'. Then I could play with Alfalfa every day.

But I didn't think Mom would agree to move to Montana.

The second solution, the more likely one, was for me to get a dog of my own.

I wasn't picky. I'd have taken just about any dog. We could adopt a quiet dog or a barking dog, a grumpy dog or a happy dog, a sitting dog or a running dog, a shaggy dog or a hairless dog. Mom wasn't exactly a pet person, though. She didn't love dogs or cats or anything. I needed help convincing her.

I needed Lexi.

I couldn't believe Lexi and I were related, to be totally honest. We were barely alike. She had long, straight hair.

Mine was short and curly — Mom called it *unruly*. Lexi spent hours picking out her clothes, and I just wore whatever jeans and T-shirt were on my floor, usually because I missed the hamper. She got As in school. I got grades that shared the same alphabet as As, but were a few letters later. Most of all, I wasn't annoying, and Lexi was the most annoying person in the world.

But while Lexi wasn't good for much, she was good at winning Mom over. Something I wasn't so good at. Usually, I hated that about Lexi. But not now. Because with my sister on my side, we could convince Mom in a nanosecond that the family should get a dog.

I found Lexi on her bed reading a magazine. It was one of those magazines with some annoying teen singer on the cover. The kind of magazine I wouldn't read if you tied me up and forced me to eat horseradish.

Have you ever eaten horseradish? If you have, you know what I'm talking about. If you haven't, don't. You've been warned.

"Lexi, we need to talk," I said, stepping into her room.

"You didn't knock." She didn't even look up.

"The door was open."

"Did someone say something?" She continued reading her magazine. "There can't be anyone here, because I didn't hear a knock first."

So I walked backward out of my annoying sister's room and knocked. Now wasn't the time to argue. There would be plenty of time to call her names after we had a dog.

"Yes, baby brother?" she sang. She liked to call me *baby brother* because she knew it bothered me.

"I'm not a baby!" I barked. Then I took a deep breath, reminding myself that I needed to ignore Lexi's annoyingness if I wanted to get her on board.

Lexi put down her magazine while I explained what I wanted. Lexi and I argued about a lot of things. Actually we argued about everything. But I knew we couldn't argue about getting a dog. Who wouldn't want a dog?

Apparently, Lexi wouldn't want a dog.

"No way." She shook her head. "Dogs smell. They're dirty. They lick everything. I'm not cleaning up after it goes outside — that's just gross. Cats are much better pets. Everyone knows that."

But everyone did *not* know cats were better pets than dogs, because it wasn't true. Just because Lexi was twelve, a measly year older than me, she thought she knew everything. Which also wasn't true. I should have known she'd cause trouble.

"Dogs are loyal. They're fun. They're your best friends. A dog will do anything for you," I said. "He'll lay his life down for you. But a cat? You're lucky if a cat gives you the time of day. They act all high-and-mighty like they're better than everyone. Just like certain sisters." Sure, I wanted Lexi on my side, but a guy needs to stand by his principles.

"That's because cats are smart," said Lexi. "Just like certain sisters. We are so not getting a dog." She picked up her magazine again, ignoring me.

"We are so not getting a cat," I growled.

Lexi smirked from behind her magazine. I knew that smirk. It meant she was up to no good. It meant she was hatching a plan. "We'll see," she said, turning the page and continuing her reading, as if I were invisible and not standing in her room, balling my fists in anger.

I wheeled around, stomped out of the room as loudly as I could, and slammed the door behind me. There was nothing to "see." We were not getting a cat; we were getting a dog. We needed a dog. This wasn't just an everyday argument, like who got to eat the last bowl of ice cream or who got to use the bathroom first. It wasn't even an argument about who sat on the passenger side of the backseat of Dad's car. That was the better side because there was more legroom. No, this was big. It was bigger than big. It was humongous. This was the difference between right (dogs) and wrong (cats). Between getting a true-blue friend or an annoying, stuck-up hair ball. This wasn't your simple, everyday disagreement.

This was war.

CHAPTER 2

I wasn't going to just jog up to Mom and demand we get a dog. I'd made the mistake of blindly nagging her for things before, like the ill-fated trampoline grovel from last summer. No, I needed to be ready. I needed to have my case down pat and my facts on straight. Like Lexi would. So I practiced responses for all the objections Mom might raise. She wanted a dog that didn't shed? Some dogs barely shed at all, like Yorkshire terriers or poodles. Mom wanted a quiet dog? A bunch of dogs are mostly quiet, like bulldogs. Mom wanted protection against burglars? I could name a million great guard dogs.

So when Mom got home from work and started making dinner, I was ready to strike. The time was right. She was alone. She didn't seem to be in a bad mood since she was humming a song I didn't know. I rolled up my sleeves, took a deep breath, and laid out my perfectly practiced plea.

"Mom? Got a second?" She stopped humming, and I went through my list of reasons we needed a dog, the joy of owning one, the fun we would have, how they're great friends and she would love playing with a dog as much as me. "And that is why we should get a dog," I concluded, a big grin spread over my face. There was no way Mom could turn me down after that speech.

"Absolutely not," said Mom.

Mom still wore her nurse's uniform from work. She was probably tired from a long day standing on her feet. I should have waited. I should have brought flowers. I should have offered to set the table, complimented her hair, and generally buttered her up. I hadn't thought of all the angles.

But I needed to talk to her before Lexi came home. I still didn't trust my sister's smirk from the day before.

It was too late to rewind, so I pressed forward. "Why not? You won't have to do anything. I'll feed him twice a day. I'll let him out. I'll clean up after him. I'm responsible."

After dumping spaghetti into the pot of boiling water, Mom shook her head. Head shaking is never a good response when you ask for something. "Did you hang your jacket up like you're supposed to?"

I leaned back and peeked into the hallway. My spring coat lay in a heap next to the front door, which is where I usually threw it.

"No," I admitted.

"Did you put your shoes away?" asked Mom.

My shoes were under my jacket.

"No," I repeated.

"Then how can I trust you to take care of a dog?"

"Because a dog isn't a jacket or shoes. He's your best friend. And I wouldn't leave my best friend in the hallway. And if I did, dogs have feet. He'd just run over to the kitchen." I could be responsible. I could! I trotted to the front hall and picked up my shoes and jacket. "See? I'm putting these away right now."

I marched my stuff — very responsibly — into the mudroom. Mom watched closely as I tossed them inside. I wiped my hands and shouted, "Ta-da!"

"The coat goes on a hook. The shoes go in the shoe bin." She sighed.

"I know that," I muttered. "I was doing that next." Not really. But I hung up the coat and put my shoes in the shoe bin, nice and neat. "Now can I have a dog?"

"Absolutely not."

Which means I cleaned up for no reason at all. But I couldn't give up. This was too important. I didn't just want a dog. I needed a dog.

The front door swung open and Lexi strolled in. Without a word, she glided into the mudroom, where she hung up her coat and placed her shoes in the bin. Then she said in her most annoyingly fake-sweet voice, "Mom, can we get a cat?" She threw me one of her smirks. I cringed.

"Absolutely not."

Now it was my turn to smirk.

"Please! I'll take care of the cat all by myself," she pleaded. "I'm responsible."

Mom arched her eyebrow. Her left eyebrow, to be exact, which is pretty impressive. I've tried to arch one of my eyebrows, but I can't. You'd think something like eyebrow arching would be hereditary. Apparently it's a talent that wasn't passed on to me. I blame Dad.

"I know you are responsible," Mom said as she stirred the spaghetti in the pot. "How's cheerleading going?"

"Cheerleading?" asked Lexi. "Mom, you know I quit cheerleading."

"And how's choir at school?"

"Mom, you know I quit choir."

"And how is ice-skating? And softball?"

"Mom, you know I quit . . ." Lexi quieted and scrunched up her lips. She furrowed her brow. "Okay. Fine. I get the point. But I'm not going to quit a cat."

"How do I know that?"

"Because it's an adorable, furry kitten that will depend on me. That is way different than ice-skating lessons."

"Ice-skating lessons that cost a lot of money," said Mom as she lifted the pot of spaghetti and drained it in the colander. A big cloud of steam filled the sink.

"That wasn't my fault," Lexi protested. "The teacher was a tyrant. But imagine how cute and fuzzy little kittens are!"

"A cute kitten that will turn into a not-as-cute cat. And then who's going to be stuck caring for it while you're on to the next thing?" asked Mom as she plopped the pasta into a serving bowl.

"But a cat is different."

"How?"

Lexi smiled with her Little-Miss-Perfect smile, the smile that had everyone in the world fooled, except me. The smile was worse than the smirk, because the smile meant she knew something I didn't. It meant she had a plan. "I have charts."

More evil words have never been spoken.

"After dinner," said Mom. "Let's eat!" She hoisted the pasta bowl and carried it over to the kitchen table. But my appetite was disappearing as quickly as the steam rising from the bowl of spaghetti.

CHAPTER 3

After dinner, Lexi propped open her easel in the family room and began organizing a whole assortment of poster boards. I knew I had to act fast. I cornered Mom in the kitchen.

"Dogs are great exercise," I pointed out. "By walking them every day you sweat off the pounds!" Mom threw me a dirty look. "Not that you need to lose weight. You look great!" From her continued frown I knew I needed to change tactics. "Some dogs don't shed!" I added, reaching into my bag of dog tricks. "And some are really quiet. We can get one of those."

Mom didn't seem impressed. She tried to sidestep around me and out of the kitchen, but I moved in front of her again. I quickly shifted to Plan B. Or maybe Plan F. I didn't really have them lettered.

"Please, please, please!" I begged. Begging didn't usually work with Mom, but I was desperate.

"Excuse me," Mom said, still attempting to walk around me. But I wasn't budging.

"I'll do anything. I'll mow the lawn. I'll cook dinner. I won't hang up just my coat, but your coat. I'll make my bed. I'll make Lexi's bed." Mom arched her left eyebrow. "Okay, I won't make Lexi's bed, but that's only because she wouldn't want me in her room without permission."

Mom tried to wriggle past me once more, but she wasn't going anywhere. Not yet. "It's not fair!" I moaned. "You never get me what I want. You wouldn't let me buy Grand Theft Zombie Fighters last month, or those basketball sneakers, or let me paint my room, or anything!"

Mom frowned. "The sneakers cost two hundred dollars, and there are more important things to spend money on." I doubted that. "That video game was too violent. And you are not painting your room in blue, green, and yellow stripes, end of story." I got on my knees to grovel, but this turned out to be a mistake. Mom easily walked around the kneeling me and into the family room, where Lexi and her posters waited. My sister stood next to her easel. It propped up a sign that read:

WHY WE SHOULD GET A CAT

A PRESENTATION IN VIVID COLOR BY LEXI

Gold and silver glitter covered the poster. The letters were stenciled and painted in bright colors. And it had — I hate to admit this — a really impressive drawing of a cat. Lexi might have been annoying, and wrong about pets, but she made excellent posters.

"Why we should get a cat. Presented by me." Lexi cleared her throat. She removed the first poster from the easel, revealing the board behind it. "Item number one. Cats are quiet."

The poster was titled: HUSH! THE QUIET CAT. She must have used an entire tube of glitter glue on it. The board listed the noise levels, in decibels, of a rocket launch, a thunderclap, a rock concert, a dog bark, a lawn mower, a soft whisper, and a cat. Guess which was the quietest?

"As you can see," Lexi lectured, pointing to the board, "the average cat purr is quieter than even a soft whisper. Compare that to a dog's bark, which can be as loud as a power tool."

"Some of us like the sound of power tools," I argued. Lexi rolled her eyes.

I sat on the sofa with my arms crossed as Lexi took Mom through a series of posters, each with more glitter than the last. They covered various cat topics, including THE INDEPENDENT CAT; CATS AND MICE: A HISTORY; and CAT GOT YOUR TONGUE? CATS AND CLEANLINESS. Sure, cats might not need to be walked. But so what? Walking a dog is fun, if it's not raining or cold. Cats chase away mice and rodents, but I was almost positive we didn't have a mouse problem. And sure, cats give themselves tongue baths, but isn't that sort of gross if you think about it?

Still, Mom nodded the entire time. Head nods are not a good sign when they're working against you.

I don't know how Lexi found time to create six posters, each loaded with silver and gold glitter, painted pictures, and elaborately detailed statistics. But things were looking bleaker for me with every poster.

I did not want to live with a cat. I was not going to live with a cat. No way, no how.

"Very nice presentation, Lexi," praised Mom, followed by more head nods. I felt a large lump growing in my throat. "You put a lot of work into this." Lexi beamed and I wanted to throw up. "But I have some questions."

Lexi gulped and my lump shrunk. Mom asking questions was a good sign. It meant she wasn't convinced. It meant I had a sliver of hope after all: a small, rice-sized sliver, but still a sliver.

Mom turned and looked at me, too. "I have questions for both of you."

My lump grew back, extra large.

CHapteR 4

"**A**sk away," said Lexi. She stood straight, trying to look calm and confident, but Mom was famous for her tough questions. Her questions were even worse than a math teacher asking you a problem involving trains, distance, starting times, and when the trains would pass each other assuming one traveled forty-five miles per hour in an easterly direction and the other traveled thirty miles per hour in a westerly direction. I mean, when would I ever need to know what time two trains pass? Teachers had too much time on their hands if they were coming up with questions like that.

"What happens to the pet when you two visit your dad for the weekend?" Mom asked. "I'm not going to take care of it while you're away."

"Dad loves cats," said Lexi. Mom arched her eyebrow again. "He'll grow to love them, at least. Everyone loves cats! I'm sure Dad will be happy to let Fluffernutter stay over with us."

"Fluffernutter?" asked Mom, scratching her head.

"That's what I thought we might name her," mumbled Lexi, blushing slightly. She shuffled through a thick notepad. "I started making a chart of cat names but ran out of time. I have a list somewhere. . . ."

"But Dad loves dogs more," I jumped into the argument while Lexi was distracted. "He wanted a dog when he was growing up. He told me that once. I bet he'd love a dog, and I'll even let you and Dad name it. You can name it something way cooler than Fluffernutter."

Score one for me.

Mom neither smiled nor frowned. She was as easy to read as a math textbook. "I have another question," she said. "Who's going to pay for it? Pets are expensive and money doesn't grow on trees, you know."

"I'll get a job," I said before Lexi could answer. I had thought this one out already. "And I'll pay for the dog myself out of my earnings. The dog, I should add, that you and Dad get to name something other than Fluffernutter."

Mom still looked dead serious. She wasn't yet convinced. "I don't know. It's not a one-time price. There are vet bills and food and a lot of other costs. And who's going to hire an eleven-year-old kid?"

"A lot of people," I said. "I can do all sorts of things to make money. And I'll keep my job even after we get a dog so I can continue to pay for it."

"I'm not sure," Mom mumbled to herself. But she didn't leave the couch and she didn't shake her head. She was softening like an overripe banana. "How will you have time for a job and play soccer, and hang out with your friends and keep up with your schoolwork? You're already struggling in math."

"I can do this, Mom. I know I can. Trust me." I flashed my brightest smile. "I can be responsible."

Mom was silent. Mulling things over. I had a good feeling about this. It was going to happen. My own dog!

"If your grades slip, or if you get too busy, we would have to get rid of it," said Mom.

"But they won't. I'll study extra hard, I promise. You'll love a dog, Mom. I bet the dog, whose name isn't Fluffernutter, will be your best friend!" I couldn't believe it. I had beat Lexi and her stupid posters. I never beat Lexi at anything. I felt so happy I could almost burst, a balloon of joy being filled with helium and floating up and up and up to the ceiling.

"Wait a second," said Lexi. "I have an idea." She smiled, and just like that, a toothpick pricked my helium balloon of happiness. It flittered helplessly all around the room before finally landing on the floor, a worthless heap of rubber. "I think Otto trying to earn enough money for a pet is a great idea."

If I could have arched my eyebrow, this would have been the ideal time for it. Instead, I furrowed my forehead, which is the next best thing. "You do?"

"What better way to show Mom you can be responsible? Of course, if you can't earn enough money it would be a shame. Especially since owning a cat costs way less money than owning a dog."

"How much less?" asked Mom, leaning forward.

Lexi pulled down poster number six to reveal a final poster. It was coated with glitter an inch thick. It had little red hearts and a bright green, three-dimensional dollar sign. She had spent a lot of time on *this* board. "I call your attention to chart number seven!" She waved at it broadly, like a ringmaster introducing trained seals. "I bring you: PETS AND MONEY. OR: WHY DOGS ARE REALLY, REALLY TOO EXPENSIVE."

Lexi had written down categories with dollar amounts separated in columns for dogs and cats. "As you can see," she said, pointing to the first column on the board, "dogs have much higher vet bills compared to cats. Look how much money it costs for vaccines, heartworm medication, dog food, a doghouse, and so on. Owning a dog costs a small fortune!" She pointed to the second column. "Now look at how much less it costs to own a cat. Food is less. Medical costs are less." She tapped the bottom of the board, where the totals were written in bold numbers. "In conclusion, the total cost of caring for an average-sized dog is more than one thousand five hundred dollars a year, compared to less than a thousand dollars a year for a cat."

"But it doesn't matter," I protested. "I'm going to work for the money."

"Exactly," said Lexi. "And I know you can raise the money." She said this in such a sweet, smiling voice that I knew she was lying through her teeth. "But what if you can't? I propose a small contest. We each raise money for our pet. Whoever raises it soonest, wins. Of course, Otto will need to earn a lot more money, since dogs cost so much more. It's only fair."

"That's not fair!" I complained. "It's not my fault dogs are twice as expensive."

"They're only fifty percent more expensive, math genius," Lexi scoffed. "And you're the one that wants a pricier pet."

"Dogs cost more because they're better animals. Nice cars cost more than cheap cars. Nice houses cost more than lousy houses. Dogs cost more than disgusting cats because they're better." I mean, everyone knows that, and Mom shouldn't need to read a stupid poster to know it. I was so angry, I could feel my face burning red.

"Dogs are not better. Dogs have horrible breath. They just ooze smell. Do we really want a walking stink bomb in this house?" asked Lexi, wincing.

"Why not? We already have you!" I yelled.

"It's called perfume!" Lexi screamed back. "And it's a mix of honeysuckle, green apple, vanilla, and mandarin."

"Stink bomb! Stink bomb!"

"Knock it off!" yelled Mom. "I agree with Otto."

"You think Lexi is a stink bomb?" I asked, surprised.

Mom shook her head. "No. I agree it wouldn't be fair for you to have to earn more money. But I like the idea of a contest. Here's what we'll do. Whoever raises five hundred dollars, wins. And the winner decides what pet we get."

"But, Mom —" said Lexi.

"No *but*s," interrupted Mom. "Except for a few ground rules. You still have to do all your chores and homework. If either of your grades at school slip, you're disqualified, no matter how much money you've saved. Your father has to agree, too. And one more thing. Both of you have to share the responsibility of taking care of the winning pet, dog *or* cat. Agreed?"

"Agreed!" Lexi and I shouted at the same time.

"Today is March second. I'll give you both until the end of the month. If neither of you has raised enough money, we don't get a pet. Understood?"

I nodded my head. You bet I understood. I sprinted toward the phone to call Dad. I needed to get him on board immediately. "Your father's out of town on business," Mom called out. "You can ask him when you see him next weekend."

I skidded to a halt. Lexi snickered at me, but I couldn't wait to throw those snickers back to her hair-ball-loving face.

Lexi didn't have a chance. I could earn this money in my sleep.

Assuming someone would pay me to sleep.

I was confident I could come up with even better ideas to earn money in no time at all.

Chapter 5

SATURDAY, MARCH 3
MONEY SAVED: $0.00

Malcolm and I were in his backyard, which was just a few streets away from mine. "Watch this," I shouted, getting ready to amaze him with my soccer juggling skills.

Soccer juggling is when you bounce the ball from one foot or leg to another foot or leg without the ball hitting the ground. I once juggled a ball forty-two times in a row. No one else on my team could come close.

I bounced the ball twice on my knee: one, two . . . and then the ball careened awkwardly and landed on the grass.

"Impressive," said Malcolm, clapping.

"You're so not funny." I nudged the ball to him, but a little too hard, and it skittered past and into his bushes. "Sorry. I'm distracted, that's all. I have less than a month to raise five hundred dollars."

"So why are you playing soccer?" asked Malcolm. "Shouldn't you be out robbing a bank or something?" He bounced the ball from foot to foot. I had been teaching him how to juggle for the past few weeks, as part of my special Otto's Soccer Clinic. Malcolm was my only student. "I don't see how you're going to earn that kind of money without robbing a bank, anyway. Have you heard of Pretty Boy Floyd? You could be Ugly Face Otto."

Malcolm smiled when he said it. He was my best friend, so he was allowed to insult me. We had this game where we took turns insulting each other, but he usually won. He was better at language arts than me, too. And math. But I was better at soccer, so it all evened out. You need friends who are better than you at stuff. Then you can get them to do things, like think of ideas to earn money so you can get a dog.

"Soccer players get paid millions of dollars a year," I said. "Do you think I could find a team to sign me for five hundred dollars? That'd be a bargain."

Malcolm kneed the ball to his foot, under his leg, and then to his knee. It was a pretty nice trick. Maybe I shouldn't have taught him how to juggle so well. Then he kicked the ball back to me. Now it was my turn to show off my soccer skills. After all, I was the soccer star here. I bounced the ball twice on my left foot, hopped right, but then smacked it too hard and the ball rolled into the bushes again.

"A team wouldn't want you even if you paid *them* five hundred dollars." Malcolm giggled.

"That's so funny I forgot to laugh." I needed a plan, and maybe more soccer practice. "I can't let Lexi win. I'll never hear the end of it. I just need one great idea to raise cash and I'm set." I snapped my fingers. "I know. I could expand Otto's Soccer Clinic. Show kids how to juggle! I'd make a fortune."

I nudged the ball up on my right knee, bounced it on my left knee, my right foot, and then into the bushes yet again.

I really needed to practice.

"That's a great idea," said Malcolm. He began speaking to an imaginary group of soccer students. "Kids, watch me, and then do the opposite."

"You're not being very helpful."

"Sorry. But your ideas stink. Don't blame the messenger."

"Fart face."

"Pickle head."

"French-fry breath."

"Amoeba-brained fungus-oozing scooter head."

"Good one."

"Thanks."

See? He's a lot better than me at insults.

"But I have a moneymaking idea that you'll think is simply brilliant." I had done a little research on the computer that morning. I needed to find just the right idea: easy, well-paid, and not impossible, maybe. "Ready?" Malcolm nodded. "Are you sure?" Malcolm nodded again. "Here I go."

"Just tell me already."

"I can move to Hollywood and get my own TV show."

He stared at me. "Really? That's your genius plan? You can't act. Or dance. Or sing."

"But I have Hollywood good looks. TV actors make a mint. Or I could just get a reality show. Anyone can have one of those."

"Great idea. They could call it *The Biggest Total Loser*," Malcolm suggested with a laugh.

"I'm serious!"

"That's what scares me," said Malcolm. "You're never getting your own show. What else do you have?"

"Okay. This next one is excellent. Really." Malcolm didn't look convinced. "I could become a lawyer." Lawyers get paid like five hundred dollars an hour. I work for one hour and I'm done. But Malcolm didn't even have to respond to that last idea for me to know it was lousy.

"You need to start smaller." Malcolm juggled as he talked, barely paying attention to what he was doing, but kicking flawlessly. "How about doing work around the neighborhood?"

"You mean like real labor? It could take weeks to make five hundred dollars if I had to actually work for it."

"Then you better get started." Malcolm continued his fancy footwork. I would have to put in some extra practice time if I was going to remain the team soccer-juggling champion.

But I had to admit it. Malcolm's idea made sense. That's why they call it *earning* money. Besides, I'd do just about anything to remove that smirk from Lexi's face, even if it meant a real day's work, however awful the idea sounded. I just needed to be responsible and I'd start earning money out of my ears. Sort of like earwax, but with money.

I decided mowing lawns was the perfect way to earn money. I was wrong.

"Our lawn doesn't need to be mowed. Come back in June," said Mr. Weinstein, patting his stomach. I'm not sure why he patted his stomach. Maybe he just ate. You don't get a stomach as big as his without eating a lot. Exercise isn't really his thing. That's why I thought he would be eager for someone to mow his lawn.

The next house wasn't any better. "Aren't you a bit early in the season?" said Ms. Strepp. She didn't have kids, so I figured she'd be a sure customer. People without children love hiring kids to do stuff. I think it's because they feel guilty that other people raise kids while they go on fancy vacations all the time.

"Are you nuts? Go away," said Mr. Paris, who then closed the door on me. Mr. Paris isn't the nicest neighbor. But when you need money, you can't be choosy. Even mean people have cash.

So, maybe I hadn't thought through the lawn mowing idea very well. Finding a lawn to mow was as easy as eating horseradish, and I've already told you my feelings about horseradish. I guess March isn't the best time of year for lawn mowing. I had wasted almost an hour and a half knocking on doors and hadn't made a red cent. Or any colored cent.

I didn't know what Lexi was doing, but I wouldn't have been surprised to learn she was raking in the dough already.

Knocking on doors all day is tiring, especially when wheeling around a heavy, old lawn mower. After steering it back in our garage, I grabbed a cold bottle of soda from our fridge and practically downed it in one gulp.

But before I tossed the bottle in the trash, I couldn't help notice the words printed on the side of it:

DEPOSIT: 5¢.

That means I could get a nickel for every bottle I brought back to a store! Now, a nickel isn't a fortune, but I bet if I walked around the city I could find hundreds of empty bottles in no time. I just needed one thousand bottles and I'd be set. Or maybe I needed ten thousand bottles. I had a hard time carrying the zeros, but money was money.

"Why am I coming along?" howled Malcolm. I dragged my old red wagon behind me as we walked down the sidewalk toward the park. The wheels were really rusty and made a loud squealing racket when they rolled. So we had to yell to be heard. "I have better things to do!"

"What was that?" I asked, shouting.

"Better things to do!" he screamed. "I have better things to do!"

"Like what?"

"What?"

"Like what?"

I stopped dragging the red wagon so we could talk. "I could be doing lots of things," said Malcolm. "Brushing my teeth. Watching paint dry. Really, anything in the whole world. I'm not the one who wants a dog."

"But best friends help best friends. Do you want Lexi to win?"

"Of course not."

"Do you want to see her demolished like an old soda can, smashed into smithereens, and then thrown into a trash compactor?"

"I don't know," said Malcolm. "That sounds a bit harsh."

"Harsh? We're talking Lexi! We're talking cats! Do you want me to lose?" Malcolm shook his head. "Then let's go." I yanked the red wagon forward. If Malcolm said anything else, I couldn't hear. I think he might have groaned.

But didn't Malcolm know that this was war? War wasn't for the squeamish. It was kill or be killed! Dog eat dog! Or rather, dog eat cat.

We arrived at the park and walked down the long gravel parking lot. There were no cars. Although the park was empty, people always left bottles behind. Our family went on a picnic a few years ago — this was before Mom and Dad got divorced — and we found four bottles without even trying. Dad flew off the handle, saying litterers didn't respect the environment, and he used a bunch of other words, some not very nice. But the more people littered, the more moola for me.

Hopefully, there was an epidemic of littering going on.

Malcolm and I had the entire park to ourselves. It was a bit chilly. Maybe if it were warmer there would have been more bottles. After about twenty minutes of searching, we found one.

"This stinks!" I complained. "You'd think someone would trash the place up a bit. Why is the park so clean, anyway?"

"Some people like clean parks," said Malcolm.

"Sure. Cat lovers probably," I grumbled.

We spent the next hour walking around looking for bottles. We even walked all the way to Grand River Avenue, with its long string of stores and lots of people. There weren't humongous megastores, it wasn't that sort of downtown, but there were a couple dozen smaller places, like the Wow Cow Ice Cream Parlor, Schnood's Grocery Store, Dry Cleaner's Dry Cleaning (that's what the sign said), Hair Sensations Beauty Salon, the library, the You Pet-Cha! Pet Store, a couple of restaurants, and so on. Ever since I started middle school Mom let me bike out there. She said I wasn't old enough when I was only in fifth grade. She said it wasn't safe. I argued it wasn't safe anywhere and that a meteorite could land on me in the backyard. It could happen. Maybe.

So Mom said I couldn't play in the backyard anymore, either. Luckily, that only lasted a couple of days. Fortunately, no meteorites ever landed.

But here, it was like the town had gone green overnight. Even with searching inside trash cans and looking behind the convenience store, all we picked up were eight bottles. I may not have been great at math, but I knew I wasn't close to five hundred dollars.

"Any other bright ideas?" asked Malcolm.

"You're the one that told me to start small. This was all your plan."

"You're supposed to be the brains of the operation," he said. "Of course, you need a brain first."

"Burp head."

"Repugnant dung beetle."

"Cucumber nose."

"Squat-nosed malodorous mountain weasel."

I let the insult slide. Besides, I wasn't sure what *malodorous* meant.

But I couldn't worry about insults. I only had a few hours left in the day to find valuable employment. I had read about people without jobs and always wondered why they couldn't just get one in like three seconds. But now I knew. Finding steady work was going to be more difficult than I first believed.

"You could wash cars," suggested Malcolm. "People need their cars washed, even in March."

Which wasn't a bad idea, I had to admit. Malcolm had a knack for making cash. His dad was an accountant, and accountants are all about making money. It was probably hereditary, like my inability to arch eyebrows. I blame Dad.

"I wonder how many cars we can wash in one day?" I asked.

"We? I have to go home. It's getting late."

"Home? But what about me? You can't expect me to earn my money by myself."

"Of course I can. It's your pet. Earning money is your responsibility."

I bristled, but nodded. I was all about responsibility! And as it turned out, I didn't need Malcolm's help at all. Mr.

Willoughby, who lived across the street and four houses over, said that his car needed washing. He drove a minivan, which made it impossible for me to clean the very top of it, but you wouldn't know it unless you were a giraffe or flying a helicopter. I charged him five bucks, but he didn't have any change, so he gave me a ten. I should have charged him fifty and maybe he would have given me one hundred dollars. Oh, well. Live and learn.

"Fifty bucks to wash my car?" said Mrs. Flanders, seven doors down. "I'll give you five bucks."

"It's a deal," I said. Unfortunately, she had exact change.

I hoped I could wash one hundred cars that day, and at five bucks a pop I'd be set. But I couldn't find any more to wash, and I knocked at just about every house in the neighborhood. I even knocked on Mr. Willoughby's door again. He didn't think his car needed washing more than once in the same day. Since he had paid me ten dollars, he said I was more than welcome to wash it again for free, but I didn't. Still, I made fifteen dollars. It wasn't enough to buy a dog, but I was getting closer.

I had other tricks up my sleeve, too.

I called Grandma Sylvia when I got home. She lives in Florida, so we only see her once a year. Grandma always sends a check for fifty dollars on my birthday. I figured that just might be my ticket to fast money.

"Grandma? It's me. Otto," I said after she answered the phone.

"Otto?" Grandma gasped. "Why are you calling? Is anything wrong?" I guess I don't call her often, or ever.

"No. Just calling to say hello!" I took a deep breath. "Grandma. I need cash."

There was a pause on the line. "Excuse me?"

"Cash. I need it bad."

Grandma's voice raised two octaves. "Otto, what's going on? Are you in trouble? Where's your mother?"

"Everything's fine," I assured her. "I was just wondering if, maybe, I could get an advance on my birthday money. You send me fifty bucks every year. So I thought, instead, you could just send me five hundred dollars now. And then you're off the hook for the next ten years. Just think of all the money you'll save on stamps."

I imagined poor Lexi's wide-eyed grimace as I handed five hundred dollars to Mom, in the form of a check from Grandma.

"But your birthday isn't for another two months."

"Right. So, I'll tell you what. You can send me four hundred ninety-nine dollars now and one dollar in two months. That sounds fair."

But Grandma wasn't going for my plan at all. She insisted I put Mom on the phone. Mom ended up yelling at me and saying it was rude to ask for presents, and that I should be thankful Grandma gets me anything, and that I needed to earn money in a responsible way or the challenge was over.

I was really starting to hate that word, *responsible*.

But it was just a small setback, really. I had a lot of other great ideas. I was just getting started. I wasn't only going to earn enough money for a dog, I was going to be rich. Maybe I'd get two dogs and hire a butler to take care of them for me. Except I'd make Lexi clean up the poop.

CHaPter 6

"**Y**ou are not sawing me in half," Malcolm insisted. He shook his head and rolled his eyes and everything else you can think of doing to show he was not kidding and he thought I was insane.

"I'm not going to really saw you in half. It's magic," I insisted, flexing an old handsaw.

"Do you actually have any idea how to do this trick?" he asked, eyebrows narrowing.

"Of course. I watched a video online."

Magicians make a lot of money. One came to our school the year before and he was awesome. He made our teacher disappear. Unfortunately, he then brought her back. So his act wasn't perfect, but anything that entertaining had to pay well.

I knew what I was doing, maybe. I wore a cape from an old

Halloween costume. The Amazing Otto had a nice ring to it. And a cape and a cool name were half the trick for magicians.

I also practiced saying *hocus-pocus*. I taped some boxes together and found Dad's rusted saw from the back of the garage. I just needed a volunteer for the classic saw-someone-in-half trick. It was a guaranteed crowd-pleaser. Not that I had a crowd. But I would. Once I perfected my act. Which meant I needed Malcolm to help me practice.

Besides, he owed me for teaching him how to juggle a soccer ball so well.

"You know, I won't really saw you in half," I assured him. "It's a trick. You just need to scrunch up your body. The chances of me sawing you in half are very small as long as you scrunch up enough. I doubt I could get through your bones anyway. It's an old saw." I tapped the saw's side, and a dull and muted twang rang out.

"How about if I saw you in half?" Malcolm suggested.

"Nope. I have to do it. I'm the magician. Plus, you're shorter than me."

"I'm shorter than you by like a half an inch."

"That's half an inch less chance of being sliced in half." I lifted a pair of sneakers that had been in my closet forever. "I'll put these on the other end. People will think your feet are sticking out."

"They'll think they're stinking out," said Malcolm, holding his nose. "Those reek."

I couldn't argue. I was surprised how much nicer my room smelled after I removed the sneakers from my closet, although there were other sneakers still there that were only slightly less stinky. (This wouldn't even be an issue if Mom had just bought me the new basketball sneakers I asked for. New sneakers don't smell like anything but rubber.) "They don't smell as bad as your breath," I quipped.

"Vomit toes," he said.

"Beasty breath."

"Sneaker stinker."

"Iguana-reeking monkey-funkying stench spewer."

"I hate you." It wasn't much of a comeback, but you do what you can. Malcolm just shook his head and laughed. "Come on," I wailed. "I need an assistant!"

"Sorry. Not happening."

"Fine. Forget the saw trick." To be honest, I wasn't entirely sure Malcolm could scrunch up enough to avoid being cut in half anyway. "But this magician idea rules. I already have the cape and the name. What else do I need?"

"The ability to do a magic trick?" said Malcolm.

I shot him a dirty look. "I can do magic." I whipped my cape dramatically, very magician-like. "Do you have any money?"

"Maybe," said Malcolm, squirming.

"How much?" I held out my palm.

Malcolm slowly removed a five-dollar bill from his pocket. "This is allowance money. I'm not giving it to you. I've earned this."

"It's allowance money. That's just like free money from your parents. You earn it by breathing."

"Not true. Unlike you, I have chores. I have to clean my room. Get good grades. And I set the kitchen table every night."

"Yes, they work you to the bone," I agreed. "I don't know how you find time for yourself." I slapped my palm. "Now hand over your money. It's a trick. I'll give it right back."

Malcolm hesitated, which gave me the chance to swipe the bill from his hand. "This should be interesting," he muttered. I chose to ignore the comment. A good magician converts the doubters in the audience into believers.

"And now the amazing money trick from the Amazing Otto!" I announced. "I take this ordinary five-dollar bill." I waved it to show my audience of one. "And I rip it in half!" I tore the bill slowly, for effect.

"Hey! That's my money!" yelled Malcolm.

I scrunched the paper into a tiny ball in my palm. "And now I will magically put the two pieces together again!" I tapped the wand on my closed fist. It wasn't a real wand, just two pencils I taped together, but with a lot of masking tape it was sort of wand-like. "Hocus-pocus!" I yelled with great flourish and magician-like command. I opened my palm.

"It's still in two pieces," said Malcolm "Except now they're two scrunched up pieces."

I looked at the two tiny paper balls sitting weakly in my palm. "It worked on the video," I muttered, trying to figure out what I did wrong. It looked really simple online.

Malcolm frowned. "You owe me five dollars."

"Sorry. Maybe I can tape them back together." I sat down on the garage floor, my head in my hands. "I guess I'll have to live with a cat."

"That's the spirit! Give up!" Malcolm pumped his fist over his head. "The world needs more quitters!"

"It's not funny," I mumbled as Malcolm snorted.

But even though Malcolm was the one laughing, I didn't hear his voice — I heard Lexi's. Malcolm's mouth moved, but I imagined my sister's happy snicker bellowing out as she cradled the lumpy Fluffernutter in her arms. I heard her terrifying cackling as Fluffernutter the evil, miserable cat spat a hair ball in my face and then meowed. I shuddered.

Malcolm clapped me on the back. "Relax. We just need an idea."

Ideas are a dime a dozen. Too bad, because if they were worth more I could have sold my ideas for big money. I had a lot of them. I could throw a yard sale with all of Lexi's clothes. I could sell advertising on my soccer jersey. I could sell body parts for medical experiments.

I just didn't have any *good* ideas.

My brain started aching from thinking. But then a plan popped into my head like microwave popcorn. "A telethon!" I jumped up and raised my hand for Malcolm to slap me a joyful high five.

But Malcolm just looked at my hand and left it unslapped. It stayed up in the air, alone. "Huh?" he asked.

"A telethon. You know, when people call on the phone and donate money for stuff. They have them on television. They raise money to fight diseases and pay for TV shows." I kept my hand up, ready for slapping.

"I know what a telethon is," said Malcolm.

"Then why aren't you hitting my high five?" Malcolm didn't answer. He just kept staring at me, and I eventually lowered my hand since my arm got tired. "We would hold a dog telethon. People call in and give me money for a dog. People love dogs. They'd donate all sorts of money. I'd probably be a millionaire."

Malcolm shook his head. "You've officially lost all your marbles. I knew it was just a matter of time. No one is going to call in and give you money for a dog."

"Someone might," I said. Malcolm shook his head again.

But he was wrong. This was the sort of big idea that won pet challenges. Easy. Profitable. All I needed was a television station to broadcast our show.

"You know, telethons don't just ask for money," said Malcolm, following me inside the house as I banged the front door open. "They have entertainment. Singers, dancers, celebrities. How are you going to put on a TV show?"

"I can do magic!" From Malcolm's expression, I could tell he didn't think that was a great idea. "Those are just details, anyway. The television station will deal with that stuff. All I need is to talk with a dog lover at the station."

"Or someone completely insane."

Apparently, television stations are filled with cat lovers. No one was interested in my idea, and I called three different stations. Two of the stations hung up on me. The third one put me on hold for like ten minutes, and then some guy tried to sell me a cable television package.

"No," I said. "I don't need cable. We have cable. I want to put on a telethon."

"You want telephone service?" asked the man.

"No. A telethon. Not a telephone. So I can get a dog."

"Your dog wants a telephone?"

"Why would a dog need a telephone?" I asked, frustrated.

"How do I know? You're the one looking to buy him one."

So, that didn't go well at all. Neither did the roughly forty-two other ideas I suggested to Malcolm.

"No, no, no, no, no," said Malcolm, roughly forty-two times.

"I don't hear any great ideas coming from you."

"I'm not about to be living with a cat."

He was right, of course. I'd be the one sharing a house with an unspeakable ball of ugly, ratty fur. It was my job to come up with that single solid idea. And I needed to do it fast. The end of the month was getting closer with every passing second.

I suppose ideas aren't worth a dime a dozen. Only bad ones are. Good ones are worth a fortune. A really good one is worth five hundred dollars, at least.

"Remember. You need to think smaller," said Malcolm before he went home.

"Right," I nodded. "Smaller."

Lexi sat in the kitchen studying with a friend from school. So at least she wasn't making any money, either. Her friend left after about an hour, and then another friend came over to study. Well, *let* Lexi do homework. I wasn't going to waste time studying, not when I could be making money. I'd think smaller, and by thinking smaller I'd think of a really big idea.

But idea thinking makes you hungry. I went to the pantry to find a snack, and that's when I thought of an idea that was big, but also small.

Apples! I couldn't believe it — we had five giant bags of apples in our pantry. There must have been a hundred of them! It would take a year for Mom, Lexi, and me to eat all these. I'm not sure what Mom was thinking when she bought them. But my creative juices started flowing. Creative apple juices.

I would become the town apple tycoon.

I hauled those apple bags to the garage and loaded them into our red wagon. The apples were pretty heavy, so the wagon's wheels made an even louder scratching noise than usual. But that was okay. Ice-cream trucks made loads of money because you heard their music playing. My wheel-squawking was sort of like ice-cream truck music, except rusty and jarring and annoying.

"Apples! Ten cents an apple!" I yelled. I knew I wasn't going to suddenly get rich selling apples for ten cents a pop, but I had to start somewhere. I learned a lesson from my lousy car-washing plan. You can't charge too much money for things. It's better to give people a deal. That's how you get repeat business.

It was like a business rule. And I was the town apple tycoon, so I needed good business sense. Malcolm would be impressed.

It worked, too! People flocked to my squeaky red wagon apple cart. They were actually standing in line. A lot of people acted surprised, too.

"Just ten cents? What's the catch, kid?" said some guy in a tie.

"No catch! Just business!" I boomed.

"Ten cents? My, that's a bargain!" said a lady pushing a stroller. "Give me four, please, and keep the change."

"Thank you," I said. She handed me two quarters and I handed her four apples. "Tell your friends! Otto's Apples are the best deal in town!"

"I'll take two," said a girl in an oversized college sweatshirt.

"Here you are. If anyone asks, you got these from Otto, the apple tycoon!"

I sold all my apples in less than an hour.

I felt pretty good about myself as I wheeled my wagon home. I whistled and jangled all the change in my pocket, trying to drown out the horrid, rusty squealing of the wagon. Not that I'm a good whistler. But I try. Whistling is hereditary, I think. I blame Dad.

I entered the house, kicked off my shoes, dropped my jacket on the ground, and then saw Mom standing in my way just outside the mudroom. She had her arms crossed, but her face looked even crosser. Immediately I could tell I was on thin ice, and that ice was cracking quickly. "Where are my apples?" asked Mom.

"I sold them?" I squirmed. You would have thought I said

something like, "I sold Lexi to the circus." (That wasn't a bad idea, except I couldn't imagine anyone paying more than five dollars for her, so it wouldn't be worth the effort.) Mom's already-red face turned redder. The veins in her neck popped out a little. "Those apples were for the hospital. To make apple pies. They're having a fundraiser. I needed to drop them off today." If she were a dog, she would have bared her teeth.

"Oh," I said in a tiny voice. "Kind of funny that I sold them, huh?" I gave a small smile.

But I don't think Mom thought it was funny at all, and I quickly stopped smiling.

"What am I supposed to do now?" she demanded. "Why would I have so many apples in the house if they weren't for something important?"

I hung my head and looked at my socks and away from Mom's eyes. Her eyes had a way of making you feel even guiltier than you did already, and I felt pretty guilty. "Sorry?"

Mom took a deep breath. "Otto, I think it's great that you're looking for creative ways to make money. But not if it's going to cost me more money, understand? You're going to have to pay me back for those apples. Otherwise it wouldn't be fair. How much did you sell them for?"

"Ten cents each."

Mom's frown grew more frown-ier. "Ten cents? What were you thinking?"

"That I'd become an apple tycoon?" I whimpered.

"I'm going to buy more apples and you're going to pay me back every cent. But apples cost a lot more than ten cents each."

"But I'm trying to save five hundred dollars. Not spend five hundred dollars," I whined.

"Then you better start thinking of ways to earn money that doesn't cost me any." She walked away in a huff. Before she turned the corner she yelled back, "And hang up your jacket and put your shoes away! They don't belong on the floor!"

"Sorry!" I called again.

Mom stomped off and I spied Lexi in the kitchen, smirking at me. I hated that Lexi smirk. I would knock it off her face all the way to Timbuktu, and everyone knows that's really far away. I'm not sure where it is, exactly. Geography isn't my best subject. But I don't really have a best subject, unless you count lunch.

I'd earn my pet dog money, and I'd wipe away Lexi's snarky smiles like they were specks of dirt and I was a bottle of hand sanitizer. "Just you wait," I mumbled as I brushed past her. She giggled back.

That night, I called Malcolm and told him about my problems. That's what friends are for — to help you think of moneymaking ideas and hear you complain about things.

"You have to consider the cost of production. It's simple economics," he said.

"Doesn't sound so simple to me." I stifled a yawn. I couldn't think of too many things more boring than economics.

"It *is* simple," he insisted. "You have to figure out how much something costs. And then sell it for more."

"So selling our silverware for twenty-five cents a fork? Not a good idea?"

"Probably not."

After we hung up I had plenty to think about. I grabbed a notebook from my desk and began filling it up with excellent ideas, each which cost practically nothing.

I could sell dirt.

I could sell air.

I could sell soap scum.

Okay, maybe not all my ideas were genius-level. But I kept writing new ones down. Eventually, I'd think of the perfect plan.

I could sell dryer lint.

I could sell the hopes and dreams of kids who just want a dog and not a stupid cat.

I kept on writing.

CHAPTER 7

After school, I thought more about what Malcolm had been talking about. Think cost of production. Think smaller.

There aren't a whole lot of things smaller than cookies. They're even smaller than apples, not including those enormous black-and-white cookies at Schnood's Grocery Store. Mom only gets those on special occasions, which means not often enough. Apparently my getting a haircut isn't a "special occasion." But I usually get a lot of hair snipped off. That should count for something.

Here's a list of other occasions I think are cookie-worthy and Mom doesn't:

Dentist appointments
I ate all my vegetables without complaining
Lexi didn't annoy me all day (it's only happened twice, ever)

Our soccer team won. Or tied. Or lost barely
Just because

People love cookies. The year before, the PTA threw a
bake sale and earned more than a thousand dollars. The PTA
lady got her picture in the school newsletter and everything.
They were awful cookies, too. Most only had one chocolate
chip in them. Some didn't have any, which means technically
they weren't even chocolate chip cookies. Everyone knows a
chocolate chip cookie is only as good as the number of chips
stuffed inside it. But people didn't complain because the bake
sale was for a good cause.

Now that I think of it, I bet those stingy, no-chip PTA
cookie ladies were cat lovers.

But I would make my cookies better. I'd include lots of
chips in each. And I couldn't think of a better cause than my
getting a dog. I'd probably sell out of cookies in about five
minutes. Cookie ingredients were pretty cheap, too. Right?
I'd wash that Lexi smirk down the sink like a half-chewed
spear of broccoli.

I'd never baked anything before, but how hard could it
be? Mom was upstairs on her computer, but I would show her
how responsible I was by baking my fantastically perfect
cookies by myself.

We had all the ingredients sitting in the pantry. I just

needed to mix them in a bowl and bake them. I'd have to be an idiot to mess this job up.

But apparently you have to be a math genius to bake stuff. I found a recipe in a cookbook that looked easy but only made thirty-six cookies. I'd need at least one hundred cookies to make any real money. But thirty-six goes into one hundred how many times, carry the denominator, minus something or other, and assuming a train is traveling forty-five miles per hour in an easterly direction, and so on.

So I didn't know how much of everything I needed. But I was going to throw in plenty of chocolate chips — more than one for every cookie. Take that, cat-loving PTA ladies!

The PTA called their cookies the "Amazing Curriculum Cookies" because the money went toward school curriculum. It was a lousy name, almost as lousy as the name Fluffernutter. Almost. Because there is no name worse than Fluffernutter.

But I could do way better. Names are important. Like horseradish — you'd think it would taste like a horse and a radish, mixed up. They should name it Jelly Bean Sundae. Then maybe people would like it more.

No. Scratch that. No one would like horseradish more, no matter what you called it.

So I started thinking of cookie names.

"Otto's Chocolate Chip Cookies!"

Boring.

"Otto's Amazing Chocolaty Chip Delights."

Better.

"Otto's Amazingly Delightful Chocolaty Chip Canine Cookie Confections."

Bingo!

Everyone loves animal cookies almost as much as they love chocolate chip cookies. I could make chocolate chip cookies that looked like dogs. The idea was pure genius. I bet this is how Thomas Edison felt when he invented the lightbulb.

When people think of great ideas in comics, they have lightbulbs drawn over their heads. What did people draw before Thomas Edison came around? Torches?

Anyway, I didn't have time to think about ancient history all day. I needed to get to work.

Lexi wasn't the only artist in the family. I would paint pictures of dogs on every cookie with Mom's icing tubes. They'd be so artistically excellent that Lexi would be begging me to make her posters for her!

"Otto's Amazingly Delightful Chocolaty Chip Canine Cookie Confections. Two Chips per Cookie."

Two chips! Take *that*, Lexi.

I looked at the recipe. I needed to melt butter. So I put two sticks in the microwave. I also took out the other ingredients: sugar, flour, vanilla extract, and, of course, chocolate chips. I removed Mom's giant mixing bowl from beneath the counter and prepared to get to work.

I'd make a hundred and one cookies. A hundred to sell, and one to eat. Or maybe ninety-nine to sell and two to eat. I'd play it by ear.

Mom had a brand-new bag of flour. It was hard to open, so I had to tug the ends and give it a rip. You would think the flour people could make bags easier to open. The entire side tore in half. Flour exploded everywhere: on the floor, on me, on the walls, and even on the ceiling. How does flour get on a ceiling? But ceilings are white, so you couldn't really see it unless you squinted.

I scooped what I could off the floor and into the mixing bowl. Luckily, flour comes in big bags, so there was plenty to scoop.

Then the microwave beeped. I have some advice: If you microwave butter, use a bowl.

Luckily, Mom had two more sticks.

I dumped all the ingredients into the mixing bowl, except for the chips. I was saving those. The recipe called for two and a half cups of flour. I threw in six cups. The recipe called for a teaspoon of vanilla extract. I poured in four. Or maybe I put in four tablespoons, I wasn't sure. The recipe called for a cup of sugar, but everyone loves sugar, so I just dumped in about half the bag. Sugar's the best food ever.

I mixed and stirred and then rolled the cookies into balls and flattened them onto our cookies sheets. Then it was time for the best part: my incredible dog pictures. After all, these weren't just cookies. They were Otto's Amazingly Delightful Chocolaty Chip Canine Cookie Confections. Two Chips per Cookie.

The chips were the eyes, and since dogs have two eyes, that's where the two chips came in. Brilliant, right? We had five different icing tubes and I used them all: red icing for the dog's nose, green icing for its mouth, blue icing for its ears, yellow for its leash, and purple just to add purple.

I know dogs don't have blue ears or green mouths. In the art world you can do practically anything. It's called artistic license. It's not like a driver's license, though. Moms don't get mad if you draw stuff, but drive the car down the driveway and they ground you for two weeks.

I want to know what genius designed icing tubes. It wasn't Thomas Edison, that's for sure. You have to squeeze hard, and then the icing plops out and makes a mess. My dog designs looked like blobs of random colors, with two chocolate chips in the middle.

I would have to change the name, since there was nothing dog-like about my cookies anymore. I grabbed my notebook to write down new ideas.

"Otto's Amazingly Delightful Randomly Colored Cookie Confections."

"Otto's Amazingly Delightful Kaleidoscope Colorful Cookies Except Those That Are Just Yellow."

"Otto's Amazingly Delightful Cookies With Icing Splotches That Look Sort of Like Dogs If You Squint. Maybe."

I didn't like any of those choices as much as my canine cookie name, but you do what you can. I put the cookie sheets with their cookie blobs in the preheated oven.

Since I didn't have a great dog theme, I'd make some great signs. Lexi would be way jealous, too. I walked over to the downstairs computer to get to work.

I typed: "Otto's Amazingly Delightful Rainbow Crazy Cookies. Two Chips per Cookie!"

Not bad.

I wanted the word *Amazingly* to look amazing, so I tried about a billion different fonts before finally picking just the right one. I thought every letter should be a different color, but I wasn't sure which colors, so I tried a billion of those, too.

It needed more stuff. Stuff people like. The list of things people like goes like this:

Dogs
Babies
Chocolate chip cookies

I put all three in my signs, which made them way better than any of Lexi's posters, even if mine didn't have glitter.

I also added a picture of a rainbow. People love rainbows, although I don't know why. If you see a rainbow, it means it just rained. If it rains, you can't play outside. If you ask me, rainbows stink.

I typed some catchy lines, too. "Be a cookie hog and I'll buy a dog!" I also wrote, "Dogs are hairy. Buy as many cookies as you can carry. Maybe we'll name our dog Larry."

I lost track of the time. Just when my signs were really looking great, I smelled something odd.

Something burning.

Oh, no!

How long were the cookies supposed to cook in the oven, anyway?

I ran back to the kitchen and opened the oven door. A dark plume of smoke filled the room. I waved away the vapors, but not before coughing about three thousand times. The cookies were burnt black, and the entire oven had a strong charred icing smell. Did the recipe say to put on the icing after they baked? Maybe. My wonderful modern art designs were now little pools of bubbling black liquid.

The thick smoke surrounded my head like clouds in a thunderstorm, and then the smoke alarm went off.

"What are you doing?" Mom yelled, running down the stairs. I could barely hear her under the nonstop siren wail. Mom held a broom and tapped a button on the ceiling alarm with the handle, and it stopped blaring. "I thought the house was on fire!" she shouted. The alarm was no longer beeping, so she really didn't have to scream anymore. I think she just yelled because that's what moms do when they're angry.

"No, only the oven was on fire," I said as a joke, but Mom wasn't in the mood for jokes. She opened the sliding glass kitchen door so smoke could seep out of the room.

None of Otto's Amazingly Delightful Rainbow Crazy Cookies were edible. I had to throw the entire batch away. I wanted to bake a second batch, but Mom said I was forbidden from using the oven again for the rest of my natural born life. I asked if she might change her mind when I was seventy-six years old, but she said there was a fat chance of that ever happening. Mom's mood was as black as burnt cookies.

"But I've made great signs!" I protested. "And I don't need to put glitter on them, like some people I know. You wouldn't want signs like those to go to waste, would you?"

She would. Mom didn't budge. She told me it was dangerous to burn food like that. It was irresponsible. And I was lucky she didn't ground me for the rest of the month.

"You can't ground me! I need to earn five hundred dollars," I complained. Mom kept her frown on. "I really like your hair today," I said, changing tactics. "And I love your shirt!" That didn't make her any happier, either.

Mom said I couldn't leave the house until I cleaned everything up, even the flour that was on everything, including me. She also told me to get the stepladder so I could wipe off the ceiling. I don't know how she even noticed that.

I held up one of the cookie sheets. "But instead of boring cookie sheets, we have Amazingly Delightful Kaleidoscope Colorfully Black Cookie Sheets," I said.

"I thought you said you could be responsible," Mom snapped.

"I am being responsible," I argued. "I'm responsible for almost setting the kitchen on fire."

Angry moms have no sense of humor.

I didn't think things could get worse, but I was wrong. After Mom gave me one more lecture about kitchen safety, and while I was scrubbing cookie sheets, Lexi walked in the room. She had been studying with friends, one after another. I guess she was done for now.

Burnt icing does not come off cookie sheets easily, by the way. Neither does burnt cookie dough.

As I scoured, Lexi wore a gloating grin. "Interesting strategy." She snickered. "Convince Mom to give you five hundred dollars or you'll burn the house down."

"That's not my plan," I huffed, using a plastic scraper to

get off a particularly stubborn, hard-crusted dough crumb. I doubt Mom would pay me five hundred dollars not to burn the house down, anyway. "I have lots of great ideas. This is just a small bump in the road to my fortune. You'll see. We are not getting a cat."

"I'd take you more seriously if your hair wasn't completely covered in flour, Snow White."

"I'm not Snow White," I grumbled, chipping away at burnt food in the sink.

"Maybe your friends the dwarves can help you. Just stay away from poisonous apples." She laughed. "Oh, that's right. You sold all of our apples yesterday!"

"I am not Snow White!" I growled, shaking my head. Unfortunately, when my head shook, a cloud of flour erupted in the air. Lexi laughed harder.

After I cleaned the kitchen, I had to shampoo my hair. Twice.

I had soccer practice every Monday night — *six thirty sharp and don't be late!* — so after dinner I rode my bike to the soccer fields behind the school. The spring season started in a few weeks. We came in second place last year and everyone on the team was back. We were aiming for the championship.

After we warmed up by kicking balls back and forth, then stretching and running laps, Coach Drago split us up into two teams for a scrimmage: the starters versus the scrubs. I was on the first team, as usual, and Malcolm on the second team, as usual. I played horribly. I missed easy shots and kept kicking the ball to the other team. Meanwhile, Malcolm had really improved, thanks to my soccer lessons. Coach Drago kept on clapping when Malcolm had the ball, and yelling at me when I had it. He told me to get my head in the game. But it's not easy getting your head in the game when you're thinking about cats and sisters and big moneymaking ideas.

We lost, and Malcolm's team celebrated like they had won the World Cup.

Coach Drago slapped Malcolm on the back and said in his thick Yugoslavian accent, "Great job. Keep up the good work and you'll be starting!" Then he looked over at me with a sort of sad, disappointed look and shook his head before marching away.

I walked off the field with my head hanging while the second teamers continued whooping and cheering.

But I'd show Coach Drago that I was still the team soccer star. I just needed to earn a whole bunch of money first. Then I could worry about soccer, schoolwork, and the rest of my life later.

I just hoped that *later* wasn't *too late*.

CHaPTeR 8

I was supposed to save money. That was the plan. But so far I'd spent more money than I'd earned. That was a million times horrible. But what made that a million, million times worse was Lexi.

While I wasted time sitting on the couch thinking of great ideas that Malcolm told me were either silly, impossible, or *what are you thinking?*, Lexi earned serious money. I thought she had just studied with friends the last two days. But I should have known something was up, especially when she smirked at me during dinner.

This is what happened: I was thinking of ideas on the couch while watching TV. I could paint houses, but I didn't own a ladder. I could put on puppet shows, but I didn't own puppets. I could fly people to the moon, except I didn't have rockets, a launching pad, or anything even remotely space-like.

I was writing down my next lousy idea, "Become an Internet hacker," when someone knocked on the front door.

"Is this where Lexi lives?" asked some large, deep-voiced, seventh-grade guy in a football jacket.

"Maybe," I answered.

"I'm here for tutoring," he said. I stared at him, clueless. "My teacher recommended her." I continued staring. "Lexi's tutoring. You know. I brought cash." He waved some bills in his hand.

I might have caught on slowly, but as soon as I saw the wad of money in his oversized paws, my eyes opened wide. "I'll take that." I held out my palm. "You have to pay in advance."

But before Mr. Football Guy could slap his money on me, Lexi hollered from upstairs, "Almost done! I'll be down in a minute! Don't give my brother any money!"

Football Guy frowned at me and put his dough in his pocket.

He waited in the hallway as I stomped to the family room. I should have known teachers would point kids in Lexi's direction. Teachers loved Little Miss Perfect because she listened in class and got straight As and raised her hand. But if you ask me, that was brownnosing.

I couldn't waste any more time watching cartoons, not if Lexi was already earning serious coin. I needed to make money, and I needed to make it quick. But it's not easy coming up with excellent moneymaking schemes when your sister is making stacks of riches all afternoon by tutoring. It's about as easy as eating horseradish without gagging.

In other words, it's practically impossible.

So I turned off the tube and called Malcolm.

"Help!" I squeaked. "Lexi's earning a fortune. Do you think we could dig for oil? Or buy a metal detector and find hidden treasure on the beach?"

"We don't live near a beach," said Malcolm.

"Which is so unfair!" I wailed.

"Listen. You just have to be smart," said Malcolm. "Think economics."

I yawned. "You're boring me again."

"No, listen. It's the law of supply and demand. Why did you sell so many apples?"

"Because I only sold them for a dime."

"Right. You supplied apples for ten cents. There was a demand for them at that price. You need to supply something people want. That they demand. At a price they want to spend. That's what economics is all about."

Supply and demand. I thought I had heard that before in school, in between naps. "I bet I could sell autographed pictures of myself."

"No one is *demanding* pictures of you."

"I could give dance lessons."

"You can't *supply* that."

"I could open a kissing booth."

"There are no *demands* for your kisses. And do you really want to *supply* that?"

"No," I admitted, trembling at the thought. "I could sell magical beans that make you fly."

A pause. "You have magical flying beans?"

"Of course not. But you're killing all my other ideas," I groaned.

"Remember, supply and demand. It's not enough that someone demands it. You have to be able to supply it, too."

After I hung up with Malcolm, I had plenty to think about. I needed ideas that people demanded! A need I could supply! I was still mulling this whole economics thing over when Lexi walked Mr. Football Guy out of the house. "See you tomorrow, Eric!" she sang. After she closed the door, Lexi flopped on the recliner across from me. "So how's it going?" she asked me.

"Awesome," I grunted.

"Well, at least you don't have to tutor some of these kids. Eric is nice and everything, but he doesn't even know the difference between a gerund and an infinitive!"

"Imagine that," I said. I had no idea what she was talking about.

Lexi laughed at my blank look. "Okay. Bad example. What are you doing to earn money?"

"Stuff," I mumbled.

She smiled. "I thought of a bunch of terrible ideas at first, like being on a reality show. Can you imagine? I'm sure your ideas are way better."

"Way better," I mumbled, looking down at my feet.

"I even thought of putting on puppet shows or magic shows. Remember when we were little kids and we put on that magic show for Mom and Dad? We were horrible. I tried to make you disappear, but you refused to sneak out of the hole in the box because you said that was cheating." She laughed, and I laughed a little bit, too. She leaned over to me. "So how *are* you going to earn money?"

I stared at her. I knew her game. She was just trying to pry for information. She wanted to get the upper hand. But I wasn't giving her anything.

"None of your business," I hissed. "I've got so many great moneymaking ideas, I don't know which one to try first."

She smiled and leaned back. "Name one idea."

"So you can steal it? No way. Just because you have some crummy tutoring jobs doesn't mean this contest is over."

"Face it, baby brother. You don't have a chance of winning and you know it," she said with a stuck-up, I'm-way-better-than-you grin.

"In your dreams!" I shouted. "It's not over — by a long shot! Don't count your kittens before they're hatched."

"Kittens don't hatch."

"Exactly! Because that's the only way a cat is coming into this house!" I howled, leaping from the couch.

"That doesn't even make sense," chortled Lexi.

"Says you!" I hollered. Her giggles followed me as I stomped up the stairs.

CHAPTER 9

My stomach twisted into shoelace knots in school the next day — the kind of knot Mom usually got out for me because she had long nails. Lexi's After School Tutoring signs plastered the hallway walls. I didn't even know the school allowed signs like those. Wasn't that against the law or something? Commerce and school should never mix, just like firecrackers and cauliflower.

Don't ask.

But maybe it was illegal. Maybe Lexi would be tossed in jail. Maybe I could hide the jail key and she would be trapped behind bars forever. Lexi couldn't earn money in prison except from making license plates. And I'm pretty sure that gig didn't pay well at all.

Lexi's signs were smothered with so much glitter and bright neon paint you couldn't ignore them even if you wanted to — and believe me, I wanted to. She'd painted pictures of books and graduation caps and pencils and even Albert Einstein. It was a pretty good picture of him. She'd gotten the hair just right, and that's the hard part.

I stared at the bloodcurdling boards, seething. When did she possibly have time to create them between tutoring and going to school? As I stewed, Ms. Gurney, the assistant principal, brushed past me. She reminded me of a giraffe, with a long neck always craning forward past her feet and casting shadows on the floor.

Class was just about to start, but this was my chance to turn the tables on Lexi. I jumped in front of the assistant principal. "Hi!"

Ms. Gurney skidded to a halt. "Yes? Hello down there." She stretched her long neck to look down at me. "Didn't see you. But I do now. I'm in a bit of a rush." She tried sidestepping me. But I sidestepped, too. Between Mom and Ms. Gurney, I was getting pretty good at sidestepping.

"Do you think those signs are a good idea?" I pointed to Lexi's glitter-covered abominations. "You can't advertise in school. It's against the law."

"Many students need studying help. I think it's wonderful that Lexi is being so industrious," Ms. Gurney trilled. "And I do not think it's against the law. Now, excuse me."

I didn't budge. I wasn't going to let Ms. Gurney go that easily. "It's dangerous. What if someone was reading a sign and walked into the wall? They could break their nose. The school could be sued. Do you want to be sued by kids with broken noses?"

"I appreciate the concern, but I don't think that's likely. I think the signs are pretty. Lexi did a wonderful job on them. She's so talented! Now, I really must go."

But Ms. Gurney wasn't leaving. Not yet. Not when every sign inched Lexi closer to a cat, and a life of misery for me. "People could be allergic to glitter," I offered.

"No one is allergic to glitter."

"The posters could fall off the wall and poke someone in the eye."

"They're not going to hurt someone."

"They could."

"Unlikely."

"What if a poster fell and then someone slipped on it? That would be dangerous."

"I really don't think that's a problem. Thomas, right?"

"My name's Otto. I'm Lexi's brother."

Ms. Gurney's face lit up like a streetlamp. "I didn't know Lexi had a brother. Lucky you! Now, get to class! I have to run! Excuse me, Otto."

Lucky me? Assistant Principal Gurney raced around me while I gagged. Finally, after the nausea went away, I stood alone in the empty hallway. The bell rang. Class started, but

I stayed put. Those posters! All those posters! I had to do something about them. I stared at one with a picture of an owl wearing exceptionally large glasses.

WHOOO WANTS TO BE SMART? YOU DO! LEXI'S AFTER SCHOOL TUTORING.

But what it really said was, "Whooo knows Otto will never get a·dog? You do! So there!"

I grabbed the glistening board, with its shining orange glitter, ripped it off the wall, and tore it in half.

That would show her!

I stood in the hallway holding the two poster halves, staring at them. I pictured Mom's eyes glaring at me as she shook her head and said, *"What have you done?"* I began to sweat. The hall was. completely noiseless except for my rapidly beating heart. I shouldn't have felt bad. This was war! Lexi had it coming to her for all her teasing and know-it-all-ness.

So why did I feel horrible, then? Why did I stand in that empty hallway gripping that torn sign, my face turning red and my stomach tied in even more complicated shoelace knots than before, knots that no one could get out, ever, even with extra-long fingernails?

I put the poster back onto the wall, carefully pressing down its still-sticky tape. But you couldn't miss the big rip in the middle. I couldn't fix that.

I dragged myself into class, my shoulders sagging. My teacher barked at me to take my seat and next time get to class on time, and he gave me a warning.

Two warnings and you get detention.

I barely heard him through the loud, yelping moan of guilt swirling inside my head. I had to ignore it. I couldn't get soft. Not now! They say all is fair in love and war. And this battle had nothing to do with love.

After school, I pedaled my bike out of my neighborhood, past the apartment complex, by the park, over the bridge, to Grand River Avenue, with its lineup of small stores.

I hoped to find a Help Wanted sign. Maybe someone needed a magician, or wanted someone to run a kissing booth. Okay, definitely not a kissing booth. I walked my bike up and down the sidewalk, and then down and up. I saw a sign asking for a busboy on a restaurant door, but the owner said I had to be twenty-one years or older. I spoke in a really deep voice and told him I was twenty-two years old, but he told me to go away. It's hard to pretend you're twenty-two when you're walking a bike and you're about eight years away from shaving.

Before I left, I pointed out the sign was for a bus*boy* not a bus*man* and it was false advertising and that he could go to jail, but I'd look the other way if he gave me a job.

He slammed the door on me.

Lastly, I walked into Schnood's Grocery Store. That was the largest store on the street. It was the only store with its own parking lot, too. I locked my bike outside, strode in, and asked to speak to the manager. As I waited, I looked at my reflection in the mirror. I had a bit of cheese cracker stuck in my teeth, so I picked it out. It's important to make a good impression when you're interviewing for a job.

That's why I wore my jeans without grass stains on the knees and a clean T-shirt. You can never overdress for a job interview.

I hadn't been in this store for about a year, ever since what Mom called the Canned Goods Catastrophe.

Schnood's has these giant pyramid displays of canned goods at the end of some of the aisles. I always wondered what would happen if I pulled out a can from the very bottom row.

The answer: Nothing good happens. If you have the urge to pull a bottom can from a giant store pyramid, don't. You've been warned.

After that, Mom said I wasn't going grocery shopping with her for the rest of my natural born life. Which raised the question: Is there such a thing as an unnatural born life, like if you're a vampire?

I hoped so, because there were a whole bunch of things I couldn't do for the rest of my natural born life. Here's a partial list I made:

Use the oven (you already know about that one)

Throw snowballs from the roof of our house

Go on the roof of our house when there is snow on it, or ever

Carry four glasses of milk to the table at one time

Use Lexi's blanket as an umbrella

Shake all the cans of soda in the refrigerator (or any can in the refrigerator)

Mr. Schnood himself came out to talk to me. He wore a butcher's apron with blood smeared on it. If you want to be a serial killer, you should work in a meat department, because no one would wonder why you walked around with blood splattered all over you.

I just hoped Mr. Schnood wouldn't recognize me from the Canned Goods Catastrophe.

"You look familiar," said Mr. Schnood. "Do I know you?"

"I don't think so," I said, coughing and looking away. "I'm looking for a job. I'm a really good worker," I squawked. "I can do magic tricks. I can even saw someone in half, maybe."

"Why would I need someone to do magic tricks?" he asked.

"I can do other things, too," I quickly added.

"We don't need any help. Sorry."

"Please!" I begged. When you can't persuade someone to do something, you should always try begging. "I'll do anything."

I think my guardian angel watched over me at that moment. It was about time, too. Because if I had a guardian angel, I think he spent most days sleeping and watching cartoons. As soon as I told Mr. Schnood I would do anything, a lady shuffled by us holding a grocery bag. She was old — wrinkly and blue-hair old — and her back creaked. In a foot race, a snail would beat her by a few laps. She hobbled to the door. It must have taken her a minute to go about ten feet.

"On second thought, you can be a bag boy," said Mr. Schnood. "You carry bags to the car for people who need help."

"Really?" I asked, excited. "I'd be great at that. I carry things all the time." It was true, too. I carried books to school, and my coat to the mudroom when I remembered, and glasses of milk to the table (as long as there were less than four). I was practically born for this job. "How much does it pay?"

In business, you need to be skilled in the art of negotiation. You don't just accept the first offer. Let's say Mr.

Schnood offered to pay me five dollars an hour. I'd tell him I wouldn't do it for less than forty dollars an hour. He'd offer ten bucks an hour, I'd go down to thirty an hour, and so on.

"I can't pay you," he said. "But you can work for tips."

"I'll take it!" I boomed. "Do you think anyone will tip me five hundred dollars?"

"I doubt it."

So it wasn't my dream job, but at least it was a way to make money. In a nanosecond I was by the side of that old, blue-haired lady shuffling slowly across the floor.

"Can I give you a hand with that, ma'am?" I asked. Old ladies love it when kids call them *ma'am*. It shows proper upbringing.

"Yes, thank you," she replied, and just like that, I had my first gig at the grocery store.

Parking lots have handicap spaces, so people who don't have legs can park close to the front door. They should have old person spots, too. Old Lady Blue Hair had parked in the very last spot in the very last row. Her bag was heavy, too. She'd bought a gallon of milk and a half a watermelon. By the time I got to her car, my arms throbbed and I panted.

She sat in the front seat and popped open the trunk, and I put the bag inside. Then I hurried over to her, cleared my throat, and held out my hand.

"Yes, young man?" she asked through the open window.

"Um, I don't get paid," I muttered. I felt greedy holding out my hand waiting for money, but you can't be too shy about this sort of thing. After all, she had a demand and I supplied it. Supply and demand. Now I demanded to get paid.

The lady nodded and turned away to start her car. I cleared my throat. "Yes?" she asked again.

"Um. I accept tips?"

"Oh, silly me!" She reached into a small change purse next to her. She gave me a nickel.

Luckily, other people weren't as cheap. You might think there would be a standard bag-boy-tipping amount. Nope. One man gave me five dollars, but most people gave me a one-dollar bill or loose change. Some people asked me how much they should tip, and I always said, "Whatever you can afford. But five hundred dollars would be great!"

They usually frowned and gave me a couple of quarters.

Money adds up fast, though. I must have helped forty people to their cars in the two and a half hours I worked. It was tiring, but when I was done, my pocket practically exploded with cash. This was the job for me.

"I'll be back at the same time tomorrow," I said to Mr. Schnood.

He squinted and scrunched his eyebrows. "You still look very familiar."

"I just have that sort of face," I blurted, hurrying off.

The next day started off even better. I got pretty good at figuring out who needed help. Old people needed assistance, as did moms with kids, people with crutches, and that sort of thing. Generally, the more miserable people looked, the more they needed me, and the more they paid. One guy with an arm in a sling and an eye patch gave me seven bucks! But a young guy in a tracksuit handed me eleven cents. I kept hoping someone would get wheeled in wearing a complete body cast. I'd be rich! But people in full body casts don't grocery shop, I guess. Still, at this rate I'd have enough money in a couple of weeks. I felt good. I felt dog-owning rich.

I'm sure Lexi wasn't making this sort of money, even with all her tutoring work. Plus, she had to help do everyone's homework. You couldn't pay me enough to do extra homework.

As I carried Mrs. Printz's bag across the parking lot, I practically heard my new dog's joyful bark and smelled his thick, cotton-soft fur. "Here, dog-not-named-Fluffernutter," I said in my head, throwing an imaginary stick and having my imaginary dog fetch it. "Good boy, good boy." My imaginary dog loved me more than anything in the world. And he hated Lexi, because my imaginary dog had excellent taste in people. We rolled around in an imaginary meadow laughing, while dog-not-named-Fluffernutter yapped in delight and then ran off to chase an imaginary butterfly.

Lost in thought, I put the bag in the backseat of the car. I walked over to the driver's side window and held out my hand.

"Young man, what are you doing?"

Mrs. Printz looked thin and weak, and it took her about five minutes to walk to her car, but you wouldn't know it from her shrill voice. It cut through the parking lot like a burning-cookie-triggered smoke alarm. She stood six cars away in front of an empty trunk, tapping her foot.

I scratched my head, confused. I wandered a few steps toward where she stood, and then the car behind me, a two-door convertible, honked and began backing out of its spot.

"Where are my groceries?" demanded Mrs. Printz, hands on hips, her voice shattering the air between us like a baseball through a bedroom window.

By the time I realized I had put the bags in the wrong car, it was too late. "Come back!" I screamed, waving at the convertible, chasing after it. But the car was already merging into traffic on Grand River Avenue. The old and shrill-voiced Mrs. Printz stood by her trunk, waiting.

"Where are my groceries?" she screeched.

"D-driving away," I stuttered, pointing to the convertible a block away and getting farther in the distance.

She yelled at me, and I bet they could hear her shouting on the moon. Astronauts probably covered their ears. She used words and phrases like *irresponsible*; *well, I never*; and *you should be fired*. And those were just the ones I could repeat without getting in trouble. After a good minute, Mr. Schnood hurried outside. He wore his white apron, streaked with blood. I'm sure Mrs. Printz wished it was my blood splattered on him.

I explained that it was an honest mistake. I put the groceries in the wrong car. It was sort of funny if you thought about it, right? But I guess Mrs. Printz didn't think it was funny one little bit. She said she would never come back. That I was a disgrace to bag boys all over the world. That unless I was fired on the spot, she would visit the store every day for the rest of her natural born life and tell everyone what a terrible place it was.

"How about if you were a vampire?" I asked. "Then that would be an unnatural born life, right?" Mrs. Printz just stared at me. I didn't repeat the question.

Mr. Schnood made me pay for the groceries out of my own pocket, which wiped out all the money I earned that day. "And you're fired," he added.

"But you're not paying me anything," I pointed out, "so you can't technically fire me, can you?" Apparently he could.

As I walked away, Mr. Schnood shouted after me. "Now I know who you are! You're that kid who ruined my canned-fruit pyramid display last year! Good riddance!"

Mr. Schnood had a pretty good memory after all.

So just like that, I needed a new job again. It wasn't my fault at all, though. It was the convertible's fault. And Lexi's, just because she's Lexi and everything is her fault.

But I needed to start earning money. If not, dog-not-named-Fluffernutter would never bark while chasing a butterfly, imaginary or otherwise. I thought about cat-named-Fluffernutter meowing in a meadow, chasing a butterfly of her own. I shuddered at the horror of it.

Chapter 10

Lexi's signs still hung from the school halls, taunting me. Their glitter reflected off the fluorescent ceiling lights like a million sparkling diamond specks of mockery. I stared at a sign featuring a worm with glasses. BE A BOOKWORM, the sign jeered. I wanted to squash it. Although, I hated to admit, the worm was pretty cute.

"This stinks," I growled to Malcolm as we stared at the revolting tutoring sign. "I should tutor kids for money."

Malcolm laughed. "Supply and demand. No one's demanding your tutoring and you couldn't supply it anyway."

"Sure I could."

Who would pay you to tutor?"

"Lots of people," I huffed.

"Name one."

Well, okay. I couldn't name anybody. "She can't win. I'll

never hear the end of it. She'll brag about Fluffernutter the rest of our lives."

"You'll try your best and —"

Malcolm didn't get it. I cut him off. "No. Trying isn't good enough. I have to win. I have to do more than win — I have to demolish her! Don't you understand? This is payback time for all the terrible things she's done."

"Like what?" mumbled Malcolm. I sensed skepticism in his voice.

"Like being born before me! And being smart! Two months ago Mom said, 'Why can't you get good grades like your sister?' Well, maybe I don't want good grades!"

Malcolm blinked. "Why wouldn't you want good grades?"

"That's not the point!" I raged. "Don't you see? There's a lifetime of wrongs here. Grades are just the tip of the iceberg with Miss I'm-More-Perfect-Than-You! I have to put her in her place! Show her who's boss!"

Malcolm shook his head. "I thought this was about getting a dog."

"Well, that, too."

As I tromped into language arts class, I overheard Mr. Corgi talking to Noah Grumb. Noah was a grade ahead of me. He was tall and played basketball. He didn't seem like the smartest guy in school, though. He always walked around with his mouth open. It's hard to look intelligent if you walk around with your mouth open. Plus, flies can swarm inside. Or drool can dribble down your chin.

It's hard to look smart with drool on you, too.

"You should call Lexi for help," suggested Mr. Corgi. "Her phone number is on those terrific signs in the hallway."

"Thanks a bunch, Mr. Corgi." Noah beamed, wiping his chin.

"Lexi is a great student," Mr. Corgi added. "She'll help you a lot."

I was sick of hearing about Miss Perfect Student everywhere I went. I grabbed Noah's arm. "She can't help," I blabbered. "She's too busy. She's closed her business. She broke her arm. She's very sick and can't get out of bed."

"I saw her in the hallway five minutes ago," said Noah.

"Well, her illness was very sudden," I explained.

I'm not sure if Noah was convinced. But much, much worse, my own teachers were recommending Lexi! Mr. Corgi, who had the last name of a dog, for heaven's sake, was helping my sister get a cat! It was hard enough living up to Little Miss Can't-Do-Anything-Wrong all day, but now this? I sat down in my seat with an angry plop.

The conversation repeated itself in my head all day, too: *You should call Lexi for help. Lexi is a great student.*

"Cheer up," said Malcolm at lunchtime.

"You're not the one facing a life with Fluffernutter," I

moaned, removing the lettuce from my turkey sandwich. Mom insists on adding lettuce to my sandwich every day, and every day I remove it. "What if Lexi came down with a terrible disease?" I added. "No one will hire her then."

"Like what?" scoffed Malcolm.

"Annoying sister-itis?"

Malcolm rolled his eyes. "It's all about supply and demand, remember? You just have to figure out what you can supply." Malcolm pointed to the lettuce lying on the table. "You're like that. Unwanted. No demand. A worn-out, dried-up piece of wilting lettuce. A senseless sprig of parsley."

"If this is your idea of a pep talk, you're not very good at it."

Malcolm just shrugged.

"But you're right. I'm parsley," I whimpered. "That's exactly what I am. I can't tutor. I can't carry grocery bags. I can't throw a telethon." I ripped a bite off my sandwich, pretending it was Lexi's head. I chewed extra hard, but I didn't feel better. I just felt worthless.

"You're good at stuff," said Malcolm.

I stared at him and scratched my chin. Then I scratched some more. "I'm drawing a blank here."

"You're good at soccer."

"Was good," I moaned.

"You're just rusty. You're a good friend."

I rolled my eyes. "Great. You want to pay me five hundred dollars?"

"And you're a pretty good writer," said Malcolm, ignoring my comment. "You got an A on that social studies report about igloos last month."

"I got a B. And you wrote half of it."

"I thought everyone got an A on that social studies report. As long as it was five pages you got an A."

"I only wrote four pages. There just isn't that much to say about igloos." I ripped off another chunk of turkey sandwich and munched unhappily.

"You're going to win. You're going to earn that money," said Malcolm.

"Then how?"

I waited for Malcolm to answer me. He didn't.

Back at home, I felt as depressed as a leaky bike tire. Mom was at work. Lexi was tutoring in the kitchen. I needed air. I grabbed my bike and rode downtown. Maybe I'd find a new Help Wanted sign. I'd do anything at this point, even a job as a horseradish taster.

I found two Help Wanted signs. But I didn't have my own car, so I couldn't be a pizza delivery guy, and I wasn't going to step foot inside the beauty salon, in case someone from school saw me. There was no way I would ever live that down.

I even looked into a couple of trash cans for returnable bottles, but I found nothing.

I dragged myself into the You Pet-Cha! Pet Store. They didn't have a Help Wanted sign out front, but I asked the manager if he had any odd jobs. He didn't. I told him that if he paid me five hundred dollars right then and there, I'd work for free for the rest of my natural born life. He still wasn't interested. That seemed like a pretty good offer to me.

But I didn't leave. I trudged past the birdcages and the fish supplies, past the lizards and cat toys, all the way, way back to where they kept the dogs. They sat in stacked cages behind a big glass wall in a small, enclosed, carpeted room. If you asked, you could play with a dog for a few minutes, before you bought one.

There were eight cages: five with dogs, and three empty ones. That meant three newly adopted dogs. Somewhere, three families happily played fetch and rolled around meadows that weren't imaginary. But not me. All the dogs here were puppies: a boxer, a dachshund, a border collie, and two golden retrievers. I focused on the golden retrievers. They reminded me of younger Alfalfas with their light brown hair.

That just made me sadder. I wondered how Alfalfa was doing. Was he happy? Had he made any doggy friends? Did anyone know which ear he liked scratched best, and how long he liked his tummy rubbed?

Probably not. Poor guy.

One of those retrievers in the cages jumped around, tongue out, excited. Just looking at it made you smile. It would be impossible to feel sad with a dog like that jumping around you all day long.

The other retriever sat in its cage, way in the back. This dog didn't move and kept its head buried in its paws. But I could see its eyes peeking out and looking at me. This was a sneaky fellow.

"Can I see that one, please?" I asked.

"His name is Thumper," said the pet store girl, a teenager with a pierced lip, a pierced eyebrow, and orange streaks in her hair. She unlocked the cage. "He doesn't really do much," she explained. "He's kind of a dud." I sat on the ground and she handed Thumper to me. He didn't move, but he snuck peeks between his flaps of fur. "His sister, Marta, is a lot more fun," said Ms. Orange Hair, gesturing to the other golden retriever still bouncing around.

"Thumper's not a dud," I said. "He's just sad." I stroked his golden fur and scratched his right ear. He seemed to like that, because he closed his eyes and squirmed into my lap a little deeper. I continued rubbing and scratching. "You'd be sad too if your sister got the attention all day. She probably gets straight As in school, and he always feels like he's second best. Right, boy?" Thumper wiggled a little bit tighter into my legs. "You'd be a lot happier if your teachers stopped comparing you to your sister all the time. And if your sister caught a disease and couldn't tutor anyone. Nothing too horrible, just one that would keep her in bed for a few weeks. I bet your sister wants a cat, too. Right?"

Thumper yawned. I'm not sure if I made him feel better, but he made me feel better.

There were a lot of great kinds of dogs. But dogs that sat quietly and made you feel better were probably the best kinds of all.

"You know what you need, boy?" I said to Thumper, staring into his dark eyes, which never seemed to blink. "You just need to figure out what you're good at. That's all. Then you'd show everyone you're better than your sister at something."

"You're sort of weird, kid," said the pet store worker.

"I bet she's a cat lover," I whispered into Thumper's ear. "And she has orange hair. So really, who's the weird one?"

Thumper nodded, I'm sure of it.

I sat with Thumper for a while, until the pet store girl told me if I wasn't buying Thumper, she needed to put him away. I gave Thumper a good-bye scratch and handed him to Miss Orange Hair.

But I felt better. The scent of dog remained on my hands, even after I got home. I loved that wonderful, rugged puppy smell. If I could sell dog smell, I'd be so rich I could buy a million dogs.

But I didn't need a million dogs. I just needed one.

I needed a dog playing peekaboo under his paws, shyly pretending not to look at me as he wiggled in my lap.

I felt low all night, especially because Lexi sat in the kitchen hour after hour, tutoring. When Noah Grumb entered the house, I groaned. It was just another reminder of my teachers working against me.

I sat on the couch trying to think of ideas, but my mind was empty. All my ideas were locked in a cage like a pet store dog. I stared at my notebook. The pages remained empty.

When Noah finally left, Lexi sat down on the couch next to me. I shot her two evil eyes. "I could tutor you on how to make money." She giggled.

"I know how to make money," I snapped. "It's all about supply and demand. I'm in a lot of demand."

"Yes, everyone wants to hire worthless baby brothers."

"I'm not a baby," I grumbled. "And this isn't over. Thumper understands. He won't let Marta beat him, and I won't let you!"

"Baby brother, I have no idea what you're talking about." Lexi leaned back on the cushions. "Where do you think we should put Fluffernutter's litter box?" She pointed to the corner of the room. "Over there?"

I felt my face turning red with anger. "I don't hear any purring in this house yet."

"Then you must not be listening. Shhh. Hear that?" I stiffened. Had she bought a cat already? "Yes, I can practically hear Fluffernutter's soft, mellow meowing as she licks her milk from her bowl."

So she didn't have a cat. Not yet. Relieved but annoyed, I jumped up. "Yeah? Yeah?" I stammered. "Well, I'll lick you!"

"Gross. You are not licking me."

"I mean in our money battle. I wouldn't actually lick you," I admitted. "That's disgusting."

"You're disgusting."

"You are."

"You are."

"You are a disgusting flea-bitten catnip-craving fur-ball freak!" I shouted. Where was Malcolm when I finally came up with a great insult?

It didn't faze Lexi, though. She laughed. "Even if I were a catnip-craving freak, I also happen to be crushing you at earning money. So you know what that makes you?" I shrugged. "Losing!" Lexi was laughing so hard she had to hold her stomach.

I marched upstairs, but her laughter lingered in my ears for so long I eventually needed to use a Q-tip to get it out.

Chapter 11

"**W**elcome to Château Dad," Dad announced as we dropped our bags on the floor of his apartment. That's what he said every time we came over. We just rolled our eyes.

Ever since my parents had split up a couple of years earlier, we stayed with Mom during the week and with Dad every other weekend. He only lived about two miles away, but it felt like going to another planet. His place was completely different from Mom's house. He was sort of a slob, and he couldn't cook, and never had anything good to eat in the pantry, and his apartment was really small, and there was no yard to play in or other kids around. But I was still excited to come over because he loved dogs, and we still needed Dad to agree to our challenge. He'd wanted a dog growing up — he told me that once. So I knew he'd be on my side. If he hated cats, this contest could be over before I had saved very much money at all.

I just needed to get on Dad's good side before we laid the news on him. I wasn't repeating the same mistake I made with Mom. I needed to sweet-talk him first. "I love what you've done with the place, Dad. Is that a new sofa?"

"No," said Dad, scratching his head. "It's the same old, worn-out couch that was in our basement for years. The same couch you've always hated because you say it smells like peas."

"I like the smell of peas now," I said. Not really. "The place looks really nice."

"Thanks, I guess," said Dad.

He didn't have a lot of furniture. The main room had a television, a recliner, a couch, and one plant: a cactus. Lexi and I had bought him a fern when he first moved, but he never watered it, so it died. The next four plants we bought him died, too. Lexi finally bought him a cactus because those hardly ever need to be watered. It still didn't look very good. Obviously, Dad wasn't a plant guy.

The sink in the kitchen was filled with dirty dishes. There was some sort of green blobby stain on the carpet that wasn't there last time we were here, too. And, yes, the couch smelled like peas.

"It just needs a woman's touch," said Lexi with a smile. "I'll clean up for you. It'll look like new."

"No. *I'll* clean up," I insisted. I couldn't let Lexi get the upper hand, like usual. Not this time.

"*I* will," growled Lexi.

"We'll see about that," I growled right back.

"Okay, baby brother."

"I'm not a baby!" I yelped.

Lexi grabbed the glass cleaner before I could, but I found some rags in Dad's closet for dusting. There was plenty to dust; I doubt Dad had ever given the apartment a thorough cleaning before. It was important that I did an excellent job, better than Lexi did, so I removed the books from the bookshelf (he only had two books so it wasn't that hard), and I dusted the picture frames (one of the frames had a picture of Lexi and me, and the other two still had the smiling couples that come with the frame when you buy it from the store). I even dusted the baseboards and the blinds, and no one ever does those. I don't even think Mom dusts those at our house.

"The kitchen looks great, Lexi," Dad said from the other room.

"I dusted the baseboards and the blinds," I yelled from the hallway. "And no one ever does those! Not even Mom!"

"Wonderful. Thank you!" Dad craned his neck to look. "But why are you dusting them with one of my best neckties?" His voice growled.

"I thought they were rags," I mumbled. "They were in a ball in your closet."

"They're my neckties for the office. They fall off the hanger a lot."

"Oh," I said, squirming. "Sorry."

Dad showed me where he kept his rags, both of them, and I finished the few remaining dust spots. His ties weren't ruined, just dusty, but I apologized about a million times, times two. I still needed to make up for my mistake. I was supposed to be buttering him up, after all. So I offered to vacuum the apartment, twice. The second time, just in case I missed something.

"I don't own a vacuum cleaner," replied Dad.

So I didn't vacuum. But I promised myself to never walk around in my bare feet at Dad's place anymore.

The bathroom needed cleaning. Lexi grabbed the disinfectant first. That was fine with me. I didn't really want to clean a toilet anyway. But I bagged Dad's garbage and straightened out his silverware drawer to keep busy.

Dad seemed to be enjoying all our work. He kept walking around, nodding his head and thanking us. Eventually, he just sat on his recliner and read a magazine.

His apartment had never been this clean, ever. I doubt any apartment in the history of apartments had ever been this clean. I sat on the couch, tired. Lexi was finishing up in the bathroom.

"So why the sudden interest in housekeeping?" Dad asked.

"No reason at all," I sang. "I just love you."

Dad said in return, "I love —" but before he could finish, Lexi rushed into the room and leapt onto the seat cushion next to mine. "Your bathroom is as good as new!" she shouted. "Need anything else done?"

"Okay. What's going on?" asked Dad, his eyes suspicious slits. "You guys don't do anything nice without a reason. Last year Otto ironed my clothes because he wanted to go to the water park." He shook his head and frowned.

"I said I was sorry," I squeaked. "I didn't know the iron would burn through your shirt."

"That's why you never leave an iron on top of clothes while you watch television."

"But there was a really good show on TV, so it wasn't completely my fault. Blame the cable TV guys. I talked to one recently. Honestly, they don't seem very bright."

"That's okay," said Dad. "It's water under the bridge. But I know you two want something. What is it?"

"Why do you think we want anything?" remarked Lexi with a fake innocent smile. "You look really handsome today, Dad."

Dad picked a crust of food off his T-shirt.

"Hey, I have an idea!" I exclaimed. "I should get a dog!"

"I have a better idea," exclaimed Lexi. "I should get a cat!"

"Cats are boring," I said. "They spend their days licking themselves and ignoring you. They don't play fetch. They don't do tricks. Man's best friend is a dog, and Dad is a man, so that means dogs are his best friend. When Dad was a kid he wanted a dog. Right?"

Dad nodded. He looked out the window as if remembering those long-lost dog-wanting days. "Grandpa and Grandma said a dog was too hard to take care of. I begged and I begged. They always said no."

"Grandpa and Grandma sure are smart!" crowed Lexi. "That's because they're older and wiser. Always listen to your elders. I bet they'd both agree that a cat is the best pet ever. They are much easier to take care of, and twice as smart, and they don't smell like dogs do."

"They smell better than you," I chirped in.

"It's perfume!" she whined.

"You smell worse than Dad's couch!" Dad threw me a dirty look. "Not that your couch smells bad, Dad." I fidgeted. "I like peas." I took a deep breath of the seat cushion behind me. "Great!" I stifled a cough and a wheeze.

"You guys want pets?" asked Dad. We nodded. "Ask your mother."

"We did already," explained Lexi. "And we're having a contest to see who can earn money the fastest. But Mom said we needed your permission, too. I'll bring my cat with me when we come to stay."

"No, I'll bring my dog!" I threw Lexi a dirty look.

"I see," murmured Dad. He scratched his chin. He examined his cuticles. "I might agree to your owning a pet. Maybe. Not sure. I need more convincing."

"I'll take care of the dog," I promised. "I'll take it on walks and feed it and everything."

"You'll love a cat," insisted Lexi. "I made some charts at home I can show you. They make good mousers, you know. They cost less than dogs, too. And then there's that smell thing." I opened my mouth to say something. Before I could, Lexi screeched, "It's perfume!"

"Both are good arguments," said Dad. "But my laundry really needs to be done. And my shoes need to be polished."

You'd think someone had lit the couch on fire the way Lexi and I bounced up. And honestly, the couch should have been set on fire years ago to get rid of that pea smell. But I snapped up Dad's shoes from his closet while Lexi grabbed the laundry basket.

"Dad's totally going to let us get a pet," said Lexi as we passed in the hallway.

I nodded. "Yeah. He's just milking this."

"Like the time we wanted to go to the movies and he made us wash his car first."

"Except I couldn't find the car wash liquid, so I used his shampoo."

"At least the car didn't get dandruff," said Lexi with a loud snort. I couldn't help but laugh, too. "But a few chores is a small price to pay for a cat."

"You mean a dog."

"A cat."

"No way," I snarled out of the side of my mouth. "You might as well surrender. You don't have a chance."

"A lot better chance than you," she snarled back, but my snarl was snarlier. "How much money have you saved?"

"Plenty. I'm up to my eyeballs in money."

"You must have eyeballs on your toes."

"We're getting a dog," I hissed.

"We're getting a cat," she squawked back, turning around and marching out of the hallway with Dad's laundry.

But I'd show her. I'd make Dad's shoes so shiny he'd buy a dog on the spot. I found the shoe polish kit he kept in a plastic bag in the back of his closet and got to work.

Dad showed me last year how to polish shoes, so I knew what I was doing. I didn't use his neckties, either, but the shoe polishing cloth he kept in the bag. I wasn't making any mistakes. This time.

I was a natural born shoe polisher. I wondered what sort of money shoe polishers made. I could open up a shoe shine stand. Except you only see those at airports, and the airport was way too far away to ride my bike. While I was on his second pair of loafers, Dad stood over me, supervising.

"Look at that shine!" I beamed, hoisting them up.

"I think we could get a dog," Dad mused, nodding. "Maybe. But you missed a spot right there." I scrubbed the side of his shoe again. "Better. But I still need convincing. Polish the other three pairs and we'll talk about getting a dog."

"Or a cat, right, Dad?" screamed Lexi from the hallway.

"Yes. Or a cat!" Dad hollered back. "If your mom thinks it's a good idea, then I guess I'm fine with it." He pointed to the shoe I was holding. "But only if those shoes are so shiny I can see my reflection in them."

"Yes, sir!" I smeared a glob of shoe polish onto another shoe. "By the way, I charge one hundred dollars a shoe."

Dad growled.

"Just kidding," I quickly added. Not really. For a moment I thought I had stumbled upon a brilliant idea.

But of course Dad would agree to a pet. I continued rubbing in shoe polish, just in case. Polishing shoes wasn't getting me any closer to earning money, though.

I could see my reflection in his shoes. And I saw a future dog owner smiling back at me.

Dad worked us to the bone. I felt a little like Cinderella, slaving for my wicked stepmother so I could attend the ball. Except having a dog was way better than going to some stupid dance party in a pumpkin.

But I still wasn't any closer to the brilliant moneymaking idea I needed. Time was dwindling quickly, too. Unless I began making money pronto, I would never earn enough cash by the end of the month.

Dad's shoes had never looked better, though. His apartment had never looked cleaner. And somehow, Lexi removed that pea smell from the couch. For all the work we did, we should have gotten a kennel full of pets.

I collected all the garbage the next morning. I didn't need to since Dad had already agreed to a pet, but I wanted to stay on his good side. Parents change their minds sometimes. Just a few weeks before, Mom agreed to let me sleep over at

Malcolm's. But then I accidentally broke a vase in the living room, and just like that, I was grounded. She said that I should know better than to play ball in the house. But she was wrong — I didn't know better.

I knew better *now*. You'd think that would count for something.

So when Dad asked me to take out the garbage, I didn't complain like I would normally. I smiled and grabbed the trash.

A large dumpster sat outside the building. All the apartment people threw their garbage in there. Trash was collected on Mondays, and since today was Sunday the dumpster already overflowed with bags in a fly-covered heap. The garbage stench was overpoweringly awful, too. Don't flies smell things? You'd think they'd prefer to whiz around a chocolate factory or something. That's where I'd hang if I were a fly.

I had to throw the bag high in the air so it would land on top of garbage mountain. Just as I let the bag go, just as it soared to the top, I heard barking. It was a sign that I was meant to win this challenge. And not a sign with glitter on it, either.

The bark was a large dog *ruff*, five rapid, deep *woofs* one after another. Across the street a lady walked a German shepherd. Golden hair. Black back. Powerful body. I bet it weighed more than the lady walking it. It strode forward quickly, as if it didn't want to be late to a dog party or somewhere else. The lady struggled to hold it back, constantly shouting, "Slow down, Racer! Not so fast, Racer! Stop that, Racer!" Each time, the German shepherd slowed for a split second and then hurried forward again.

If she wanted a slow dog, maybe she shouldn't have named it Racer.

It's not easy to walk big dogs anyway, especially when they don't listen too well. I suppose small dogs and medium dogs can be hard, too. It depends on the dog. But that's just another reason why they are so wonderful. They aren't the same. They aren't toys in a box. Dogs can be smart, laid-back, happy, grumpy, sleepy, dopey, and the rest of the seven dwarfs except for Doc, since his name didn't make any sense. It's not like the guy was a doctor or anything.

The lady could have used some help. But I couldn't waste time goofing off and walking dogs. I needed to think of a way to make money and wipe that sneaky grin off Lexi's stinky face.

And then it hit me. A lot of people need help walking their dogs. The Finches always complained about taking Alfalfa out. I enjoyed it, when they let me. It was so obvious:

What do I like to do?

Walk dogs.

What do people need?

Dog walkers.

People. Pay. Money. Walk. Dogs. Me.

It was brilliant, although not very good English. The big idea! The moneymaking plan that wasn't impossible, or crazy, or stupid, or anything other than perfect.

Supply and demand! Dogs demanded to be walked. I would supply it.

It would also be a great way to show Mom I was responsible enough to take care of a dog, since she always said how irresponsible I am. That's win-win! And it would be fun! That's win-win-win! And I bet I could earn money way faster than Lexi.

That's a quadruple win. But most important, that's a quadruple dog win.

I couldn't wait to see Lexi's face when I raked in the dough and walked my new dog through the front door. I pictured Lexi sulking in the corner, muttering the name *Fluffernutter* to herself. It was such a great picture, I wished I could frame it.

I sprinted back to Dad's apartment and went straight to his computer. I was still a little annoyed that my brilliant OTTO'S AMAZINGLY DELIGHTFUL RAINBOW CRAZY COOKIES sale signs were wasted. But I didn't need fancy lettering or colored borders or pictures of rainbows, or even Lexi's extra-glittery drawings. Because I had a great idea, and great ideas rise to the top, like inflatable pool toys.

TOO POOPED TO WALK YOUR DOG?

THEN YOU OUGHT TO CALL OTTO! RAIN OR SHINE,

I'M DEPENDABLE AND RELIABLE.

NEED A BREAK? THEN YOU OUGHTA CALL OTTO'S

DOG WALKING SERVICE!

555-1286

I printed two dozen of the signs on Dad's color printer. As the last one spit out, Dad shouted from the hallway. "Ready, Champ? It's time to go back to Mom's house."

"I sure am!" I couldn't wait to hang up my fliers around town. "Where's Lexi?"

"Your mom picked her up a couple of hours ago. She had a bunch of kids waiting for her. I think she's tutoring them. Isn't that great?"

Two hours ago? That meant she was making money while I was making signs. I felt my face turning red. I wanted to scream. I forced myself to take deep breaths and calm down.

She might have had the upper hand now, but with my You Oughta Call Otto Dog Walking Service, I'd have the upper, upper hand soon.

Dad drove me back to Mom's house, and I got to sit in the front seat. It wasn't a very nice car — old, small, and the CD player didn't work. When Dad moved out, Mom kept the good car. "You and your sister are really serious about getting a pet, aren't you?" asked Dad.

"I want a dog more than anything."

"Then you'll have to earn a lot of money." We pulled up into Mom's driveway. "Hold on," said Dad as I grabbed the handle to open the door. He reached into his jacket pocket and pulled out his wallet. He handed me a ten-dollar bill. "Don't tell your sister."

"Thanks, Dad," I said, beaming. "I'm going to win this challenge! We'll have a dog in this family!"

"I always wanted a dog. It'd be a lot of work, but it'll help you guys learn about being responsible. Good luck."

"Hey, do you have another four hundred dollars in your wallet you can give me?" Dad shot me a dirty look that said, *do-you-even-listen-when-I-talk?* "Just asking."

Dad honked to let Mom know I was home. I ran inside the house, dropped my overnight bag in the hallway, and headed to the staircase.

"Do I get a hello?" asked Mom.

"Hello," I said.

Mom pointed to my bag in the middle of the hallway. "That goes in your room."

"I was taking it upstairs," I said. Not really. I grabbed my bag and lugged it up the staircase. Just as I reached the top step, I heard purring. I stiffened. The hair on the back of my neck stood up.

A fat white cat with plush, fluffy hair walked past. It looked up at me with burning blue eyes and an arrogant, Lexi-like smirk. It purred softly. It rubbed itself against my leg.

"Fluffernutter?" I gasped. I couldn't breathe. I staggered back.

"There you are, Sasha." Avery Maples, a friend of Lexi's, walked out of Lexi's room and picked up the horrid ball of walking white fur. "Thanks for letting me bring her over," she said to Lexi, who followed her friend into the hallway. Avery stroked Sasha's coat. "Soon our cats can play together."

I glared at Lexi, and at Avery, and most of all, at Sasha. I wasn't fooled by the cat's cuddliness. I wasn't taken in by the way she purred softly in her owner's arms and batted her little eyelids. Cats were the enemy. Lexi was the enemy.

"Get used to it," Lexi snapped at me. "We'll be living with a cat soon."

"I'll never get used to a cat."

"That's a shame, because Mom says we can put her litter box in your room."

"What?" I shouted in horror, and Lexi laughed as she walked her friend downstairs.

I could still feel the lingering tingles of where the cat had rubbed against my leg. It spread through my body like an ice cube dropped down your shirt.

Time was wasting. I had less than three weeks, and I had so much money to earn.

I shouted to my mom that I was heading out and zoomed out the door with my dog walking fliers. I taped a few on lampposts in the neighborhood — people might notice them as they walked their pets. I put fliers on doors of houses that had dog toys in their yard, or had fences. I even rode my bike all the way to Grand River Avenue and put a flier on the bulletin board inside Schnood's Grocery Store, although I was careful Mr. Schnood didn't see me, and I stayed away from giant stacks of cans.

Many people tacked up signs on that bulletin board. There were ads for babysitting services, housekeeping services, used furniture, old bikes, and tutoring.

Tutoring.

One sign stood out because it was covered in glitter.

LEXI'S AFTER SCHOOL TUTORING.

It included her phone number and a drawing of some books and pencils. I taped my flier on top of it.

When I got home, I plunked my butt on the couch and put the phone on my lap. "No one is allowed on the phone!" I yelled. "I'm expecting important calls! Dozens! Maybe hundreds! All day and night!"

"Give me the phone," demanded Mom, about two minutes later. "I need to make a call."

"No way, José." I shook my head. "This phone is tied up."

"I'm not kidding. Give it to me," insisted Mom, holding her hand out.

"You're the one that won't let me get a cell phone," I complained. "All my friends have cell phones. Lexi has a cell phone."

"You'll just lose it."

"I'm responsible!"

Mom arched her eyebrow. "Your jacket is sitting in the front hallway. And you lost a shoe last month. How does someone lose a shoe?"

Losing a shoe is actually really easy. Easier than you'd think, anyway.

"When we get a dog, you'll see!" I said. "I'll be the most responsible kid in the entire world. I'll probably win responsibility awards. Trophies and stuff. Giant ones the size of my head." Still, I got up and hung my coat in the mudroom. But I held on to the phone, too.

I sat on that couch for two hours. I didn't turn on the television, since I didn't want to be distracted. I should have done homework, but I didn't think I could concentrate long enough. I was way too excited. But the phone never rang, no matter how long I stared at it, and no matter how hard I thought positive phone thoughts. I hoped my brain energy would reach out to all the dog owners in the world and make them dial our phone number.

Finally, the phone rang. I picked it up before the first ring ended.

"Otto's Dog Walking Service!" I shouted. "You oughta call Otto! And you did! Call Otto, that is." I needed to work on my phone answering skills.

"Hi, Otto. This is Mrs. Schmidt. Is your mother home?" Mrs. Schmidt was one of Mom's nurse friends.

"She is," I said, and hung up. It was rude, maybe. But I couldn't tie up the line.

A few minutes later, the phone rang again. This time I answered a little more cautiously. "Hello?"

"Is this Otto's Dog Walking Service?" said a low, muffled voice. "I want to hire someone to walk my fourteen vicious, people-hating Doberman pinschers. I can pay you five hundred dollars."

"Hi, Malcolm." I sighed.

"My mom saw your sign at the grocery store."

"Really?" I asked, perking up.

"She said it covered up a really pretty, glittery sign, so she moved it over."

I groaned. "No one has called yet." I lay down on the couch and rested the back of my hand on my forehead. "My signs have been up for over two hours. Lexi is in the kitchen tutoring someone right now," I whined.

"Want to play soccer, then?" said Malcolm.

"I'm waiting for the phone to ring with dog walking appointments. I can't."

"But you just said no one is calling. And you could use the practice."

"I said no one has called *yet*. The *yet* is an important part. They could call any second. And I don't need soccer practice," I said, lying through my teeth. "I'm a star."

"*Were* a star. You couldn't beat a potato in soccer right now."

"Sure, I could." I was pretty positive I could crush a potato in soccer. "And I'm still better than you. You couldn't beat a worm in soccer. A dead worm."

"You're a head-butting soccer butt."

"You're a dead-worm-losing soccer stinker."

"You're an uncoordinated butter-footed leather-ball-eating baboon."

I probably could have topped that insult, but I didn't want to stay on the phone too long. People might be calling any moment. "I should go."

"Good luck, ball baboon."

"Later, soccer stinker."

I waited almost a half hour for the phone to ring again. I

took a deep breath and answered. "Hello," I murmured. "This is Otto."

"Otto's Dog Walking Service? Is this the right number?" It was a lady's voice, old and cracked. I imagined an elderly woman with a cane, someone who hadn't taken her dog out for a walk in years.

"You oughta call Otto!" I blurted, my heart beating rapidly. "No dog is too big or too small."

"Hello, Otto. My name is Mrs. Linkletter. I need someone to walk Buttercup. She's very lively."

"So am I," I promised.

"Then you should be perfect. Can you come over around four o'clock tomorrow afternoon?"

I nearly leapt off my couch. My first job! And with a dog named Buttercup! I couldn't think of an easier first dog-walking assignment. But I would have been happy to walk any dog, even one named Killer, Kid Eater, or — worst of all — Fluffernutter. I could almost count my soon-to-have fortune in my head. In less than three weeks I'd have my own dog to play with and walk every day. My very own dog. And not a cat.

I'd wipe that smug smile off Lexi's face. Let her tutor the entire school if she wanted. I would win this war. I would be the best, highest-paid dog walker in the history of dog walkers. Buttercup was just the start.

So there.

CHAPTER 13

I arrived fifteen minutes early to my appointment at Buttercup's house. (I wanted to scream out: "See, Mom and Dad — I am getting the hang of this responsibility thing!") It was too early to knock at the door, though, so I walked around the block six times. I pretended to walk Buttercup. "Good girl!" I praised, and "Thatta girl!" and "Don't pee on the flowers!" Finally, at exactly four o'clock, I rang the doorbell, and forty-two seconds later the door opened.

Not that I was checking my watch every four seconds or anything.

I had pictured Mrs. Linkletter to be old and frail. She wasn't. But she was enormously wide, as if she were hiding a piano under her sweater. She had red cheeks and a tall tangle of curly hair. "Are you Otto?" she asked with her scratchy voice.

"You oughta call Otto!" I answered.

Mrs. Linkletter smiled at me. Behind Mrs. Linkletter leapt Buttercup, a white miniature poodle. She kept leaping in the air and yapping like she had just eaten ten jars of jumping beans. "As I said, she's lively."

"Just a little," I agreed.

Yap, jump, *yap*, jump.

"I have to run errands," said Mrs. Linkletter. "You'll need to walk Buttercup for at least an hour."

"No problem. I charge six dollars for thirty minutes." I had researched dog walking prices on Mom's computer the night before. I called Malcolm, too. I wanted to charge a hundred dollars a dog, but Malcolm convinced me that no one would hire me for a hundred dollars. Professional dog walkers are paid a lot more than six dollars for a half hour. But I was just starting out, so I couldn't charge higher fees. Yet.

The *yet* is always important.

Mrs. Linkletter handed me a five-dollar bill. "This is for an hour," she said. "Take it or leave it."

"I'll take it!" I couldn't be too choosy. Not until I built my dog walking moneymaking empire, at least. So I'd make an exception just this once. Mrs. Linkletter bent over and kissed Buttercup on the forehead. "Momma will be back soon," she cooed. She handed me the leash. And then Buttercup and I were off for our walk.

If Buttercup didn't eat jumping beans, maybe she had eaten a pogo stick. She leapt the entire walk. I don't know if her front paws touched the ground once. She constantly sprang up and down on her back legs.

She snapped at everything we passed, too, like people, mailboxes, butterflies, the wind, and invisible dust mites. She sprang at trees, a bush, some tulips, a candy wrapper, and, highest of all, at joggers.

"Get out much?" I asked. She just yelped and leapt in answer. "I guess not."

Buttercup was probably the most excited dog ever. "That's just a flower," I told her. And, "Really, Buttercup? Haven't you seen a bird before?"

We went to the park, which only gave her more things to yap at. She barked at the gravel in the parking lot. And at the Do Not Litter sign. And at a leaf. And at the benches, with and without people on them.

A group of kids played soccer, and we strolled closer. Well, I strolled. Buttercup jumped and yipped. There were seven guys, and I knew a couple from my team: Eric Lansing, our midfielder, and Kyle Krovitch, our goalie. Eric waved. "Otto! Hey! We could use one more!"

"I'm working!" I pointed to Buttercup, who was busy snarling at a butterfly.

"Come on! We don't have even teams. We need one more player!"

"I shouldn't!" But there's a difference between *shouldn't* and *can't*. A big difference. Besides, I needed the practice badly. I thought of Coach Drago shooting me a disappointing look as he marched away the other night. I'd show him! Buttercup could keep herself busy barking at whatever for a few minutes.

There was a tree nearby with low branches. "What do you think?" I asked Buttercup. She yapped at a gnat in response. "Do you think I could play?"

"C'mon!" yelled Eric.

"You don't mind, do you?" I asked Buttercup. She growled at a weed.

"Hurry up!" shouted Eric.

"Coming!" I walked Buttercup to the tree and wrapped the leash around the lowest branch. "Stay here, okay?" Buttercup yapped at a wisp of air. "I'll be right over there." I pointed to the game. Buttercup yapped at a daisy. "Okay? Buttercup?" *Yap, yap, yap.* So I ran over to the guys. Eric high-fived me. "I can play for ten minutes," I said, glancing back at Buttercup. She yapped and jumped at nothing.

I don't know how long we played. I scored a lucky goal, and I think we won, but we weren't really keeping score. Still, it was great to run around without having to worry about being hollered at by Coach Drago, and I could forget about sneering sisters, too. I still didn't play very well, and I missed three goals I shouldn't have missed. It was a start, though.

But the best part? I was actually getting paid for this! Sure, I was supposed to be walking Buttercup, but she was fine playing with random, make-believe insects. I bet Mom would have said I was being irresponsible. But I just felt smart.

Really smart! The possibilities were endless. I could get paid for doing homework, while walking dogs. Paid for playing ball, while walking dogs. Paid for filling Lexi's shoes with grape juice (as long as she didn't catch me), while walking dogs. This would be the best job ever.

I hadn't even heard Buttercup yap in a while. I glanced over at her tree. I bet she was napping — it must be tiring barking at everything all day.

Or not.

She was gone.

"Where are you going?" cried Eric. "Let's play another game!" I didn't answer. I could barely breathe as I ran to the tree. No leash. No Buttercup. My stomach tightened with fear.

"Buttercup?" I yelled, gulping. "Buttercup!" I shouted, louder.

Nothing. Not a yap anywhere.

My first job and I lost the dog! "Buttercup!" I screamed about ten more times, my heart racing faster and faster with each shout.

"Excuse me, have you seen a crazy, barking dog?" I asked a woman on a bench who was reading a book. She shook her head.

"Dog? Annoying? Yapping? Seen her?" I asked a jogger. But he hadn't, either.

I was in deep, deep trouble. So deep, you could dig to China and not reach it. Buttercup could be hurt. Or stuck in a tree. Or captured by dog stealers. Or one of a million horrible things.

My stomach was flittering with worry like it caged a thousand frightened moths. I kept imagining Buttercup being injured or worse. Why had I left her alone? What had I been thinking?

I hadn't been thinking, that's what.

Maybe being responsible was important.

None of the soccer kids had seen Buttercup, either. I raced around asking people if they saw an insane white miniature poodle running around.

Finally, I talked to some guy in a red sweat suit at the far end of the park. He nodded. "I think so. Over there. Jumpy thing." The guy pointed to a set of trees. I sprinted as quickly as I could, my feet pounding nearly as rapidly as my heart did. I had never run faster.

As I neared the line of trees, I heard yapping: annoying, repetitive, but wonderful, wonderful yapping.

There, right next to a tree, just at the edge of the park, was Buttercup. If she had stepped into the woods, just a few feet farther, I might never have found her. She barked at a flower, her fur up and her teeth bared. That flower was in deep trouble. I grabbed Buttercup's leash and collapsed onto the grass next to her. My legs felt like Jell-O, all wobbly and uneasy. "You scared the heck out of me, you know that?"

Yap, yap, yap. And then jump.

I had never been happier to hear a dog bark in my life.

I sat up and caught my breath, scratching Buttercup's neck in a rare non-jumping moment. My heart began to slow. I wondered if my guardian angel was watching that moment. I whispered my thanks to him.

If I was going to walk dogs, I needed to try to be more responsible.

No. Trying wasn't going to do it. I would be more responsible. End of story.

When I handed the leash back to Mrs. Linkletter, she seemed overjoyed to have Buttercup back. I didn't mention our little adventure. She gave her dog a big hug. "How was your walk?" she asked.

"Great," I croaked. "No problems."

"You're obviously a natural dog walker."

"Yep. That's me," I replied, but there was still a big bucket of guilt in my stomach. When Mrs. Linkletter gave me a one-dollar tip, the bucket got even fuller.

There were four messages for dog walking jobs waiting for me at home. I grabbed an empty notepad from the junk drawer.

And I made a special note in it:

"Took notepad from Mom. I owe her $1."

I'd keep track of what I took from Mom and pay back every cent after the contest was over. Sure, I would need the money, but this was the new, responsible Otto!

Mom and Dad would be impressed.

I called everyone who left a message right back. In the notebook I scribbled addresses and pickup times. Unfortunately, my pen ran out in the middle of the second call. I was filled up with bookings, though — as long as I could read what I wrote.

I arranged three walking jobs for the very next day. The fourth person I called back asked if I walked cats. I hung up on him.

I had soccer practice that night, but things didn't go well. Every time the ball came to me, my mind wandered back to the Buttercup disaster earlier that day, and Lexi's tutoring. She was back home tutoring kids right then, while I was playing soccer. Poorly.

I didn't play well in the park earlier, but with Drago yelling at me and Lexi's snarls flapping about my brain, I played far worse. I couldn't concentrate at all. During our scrimmage, Malcolm scored three goals, which was three more goals than me. He really looked good. Every time I made a mistake I'd look at Coach Drago, and he'd be muttering and shaking his head.

From what I could tell, he did a whole bunch of muttering and head shaking. I'd have to start playing a lot better if I was going to be our star player. Coach Drago told Malcolm to keep it up and he'd soon be starting.

We play the same position.

So I didn't like the sound of that at all.

But when I got home I saw that I had two more phone messages. I returned them and made appointments. I was too tired from practice to run upstairs and get my notebook, so I didn't write down the information until later. But I thought I wrote everything down correctly.

Lexi wasn't smirking anymore, though. In the middle of one of my calls, I caught her watching me, and I threw her a smirk of my own, although I'm not sure if I did it right. I'm not an accomplished smirker like she is. She just looked sort of confused, shrugged, and marched upstairs back to her bedroom.

I got the feeling maybe things weren't going as well for her as I'd feared.

I hoped so, anyway.

CHAPTER 14

Mom's color printer putt-putts out paper. I woke up early to print one hundred of my awesome You Oughta Call Otto fliers. I almost missed the school bus. I kept pacing as the printer spat out one copy. And another. And another. And another.

"I hope you're not using all of my ink!" yelled Mom from the kitchen.

Uh-oh. "No," I answered, although I only printed fifty-six fliers because the printer ran out of toner. I didn't know how much ink costs. I added a line to my notebook:

"Used Mom's printer cartridges: I owe her $?"

I'd need to look up cartridge costs later.

But I needed the fliers now. To be successful you have to promote yourself. I thought about hiring a blimp, but I figured those were pretty expensive, and I didn't know where you would rent a blimp. So instead I passed my fliers out everywhere. I gave them to my teachers. I passed them out to kids.

"I walk my own dog," said Sylvester Stringer when I handed him a flier.

"If you break your legs, call me!" I said.

The janitor had just mopped the floors so they were slippery. But unfortunately, Sylvester didn't fall and break anything.

I even taped fliers on the wall, many right next to Lexi's tutoring signs. My small pages looked pretty wimpy compared to her large, glittery poster boards. But I taped ten of my signs around just one of hers, which helped.

"If your dog needs walking, you oughta call Otto," I said to Tara Wilson, who was reading one of my signs.

"I don't own a dog," she said.

"Then get one," I suggested. "And then call me to walk it!"

She rolled her eyes and walked away, so I don't think she was going to get a dog anytime soon. But if she did, I bet I would have been the first person she called.

I arrived at my four o'clock appointment exactly on time, except I had told Ms. Brownstone I would be there at three thirty. Apparently I wrote down the time wrong. She grumbled but handed me the leash to Truman, a black-and-white border collie. I once read that border collies make the best

Frisbee-catching dogs. I was sure Truman would be great at it — he looked like a small ball of energy, ready to leap a mile. Maybe we could enter Frisbee-catching competitions. Those must pay serious prize money. His ears stood at attention, and he kept walking faster than me. He was a runner, no doubt about it. So when we got to the park and saw a guy tossing a Frisbee to his dog, I asked if Truman could have a turn.

"Why not?" said the guy, handing me the disc.

I waved the Frisbee under Truman's nose so he could sniff it. He wagged his tail and nuzzled his nose against the plastic edge. He was going to be an exceptional Frisbee catcher. You can tell those things. "Ready, boy?" I asked. Truman barked. "Let's show this guy what you're made of."

Frisbee dogs. Those were probably the best kinds of dogs, if you thought about it.

I hurled that disc as far as I could. I whipped that thing a mile and a half. Then I let go of the leash. Truman took off like a jet plane, except with loud barks instead of loud engines.

"Go, boy, go!" I screamed.

Truman kept running. And running. And running.

"Come back, boy, come back," I whimpered.

I sprinted after him. I couldn't believe I had another runaway dog!

I caught up with Truman a block away. He sat under a tree, panting, as if nothing had happened. With no Frisbee in sight.

I wasn't taking any chances with my next dog, Jetson. The responsible Otto didn't take chances. At least the mostly responsible Otto. I was forty-five minutes late picking him up because I couldn't read my writing, and I dropped Truman off late, and I stopped home for a snack. And I didn't realize how long it would take me to get from one house to the other. But Mr. Finley didn't seem to mind. At least he didn't mind too much. Jetson was a sandy-colored Labrador retriever. He was a big dog. A strong dog. A serious dog, with a serious expression. He stood straight with his chin up. He didn't seem like the type to run away. Besides, they wouldn't call them retrievers if they didn't retrieve things and bring them back, right? We could enter fetching competitions and make extra cash. But I wasn't taking any chances. Not this time. I was too responsible for that. So when I saw the perfect fetching stick next to the sidewalk, I knew I was going to toss it. But I wasn't going to let go of Jetson. I wrapped the leash around my hand. I hurled the stick as far as I could. We'd get it. Together.

"Fetch, boy!" I yelled. "Fetch!"

That went well for the first three steps, Jetson running and me sprinting alongside him, until I tripped. Jetson didn't stop, though. He dragged me behind him, my arms flailing, my legs trying to get under me but instead bouncing wildly. "Stop! Wait!" I cried, my butt skimming across the grass. "No! Ow! Please!" I bumbled, twisting to avoid a rock. But retrieving dogs love to retrieve, I guess.

We stopped two blocks later so Jetson could pee on a fire hydrant. Standing on my shaky legs, I removed the stick from his mouth. "Good boy," I panted. "Good boy."

I was done with throwing things, whether they were sticks or Frisbees or whatever. But that was okay. Fergie wasn't the Frisbee-catching or stick-fetching type anyway. She was a cream-colored, brown-spotted cockapoo. She was a shaggy little dog and looked so innocent you wanted to scratch her ears and pet, and pet, and pet her.

Innocent petting dogs. Now *those* were the best kinds of dogs, if you ask me.

Dogs attract people, especially cute, innocent-looking dogs like Fergie. Every block or so kids would run up to us and pet her. Some kids asked first. But others just started petting. Which gave me an idea of how I could make more cash, and I didn't even have to enter any fetching or catching contests.

No, this was a responsible way to earn money.

"Can I pet your dog?" asked a boy, running up. He looked to be in second grade or so. He was a bit of a mess — his shoes were untied, and he had a big blue stain on his half-tucked-in white T-shirt. But he looked perfect to me.

"What's your name, kid?" I asked.

"Fisher."

"Fisher, I'll tell you what. How'd you like to not just pet the dog, but walk her?"

"Really?" His face lit up. You'd think I had just asked if he wanted to celebrate Christmas twice a year instead of the usual once.

"Well, the You Oughta Call Otto's Dog Walking Service is having a special today. For just two dollars you can walk this dog for three whole minutes. You won't find a bargain like that just anywhere."

Fisher's happy smile immediately ducked behind a rain cloud. "I don't have two dollars."

"Then you better run home and get cash. And tell your friends. Two dollars for your very own once-in-a-lifetime dog walking experience."

I was a genius! If I had really long arms, I would have patted myself on the back. I walked Fergie back and forth for a few minutes until Fisher returned. He waved two one-dollar bills in the air. Three other boys were with him, too. They all carried money.

Fisher handed me his bills first. "Tooth fairy money," he explained.

"A smart investment, kid," I assured him. "The tooth fairy would be proud." I handed over the leash. "Here you go. Three minutes. Starting now. And whatever you do, don't let go of the leash." I started counting the seconds in my head.

Fisher had obviously never walked a dog before. He seemed nervous. He walked slowly and held the leash out as far away from him as possible.

"Relax, kid. She won't bite. Probably."

Fisher walked Fergie for only about a minute before giving the leash back to me. I collected each kid's dough while they took turns. Easy money.

After everyone had a turn I threw them a big smile. "Thanks, guys. I'll be back. Same time, tomorrow. Tell your friends. You Oughta Call Otto's Dog Walking Service — just three dollars a walk!"

"I thought it was two dollars," moaned Fisher.

"Supply and demand, kid," I said, patting my pocket, crammed with cash.

So, I felt pretty good about my first full day of business. I had money in my pocket and a moneymaking, dog-sharing side job. Now that the You Oughta Call Otto Dog Walking Service was up and running, my dog walking empire was growing by Frisbee-leaping leaps.

As I walked home, I passed Mrs. McClusky from down the street, unloading grocery bags from her car. Mrs. McClusky lived by herself and was pretty old. The bags looked heavy. But as you know, I was pretty good at bag carrying from my Schnood's Grocery Store days.

So I carried her last bag into the kitchen, and I didn't even ask to be paid for helping. That's because the new, responsible Otto did nice things for people.

The new, responsible Otto didn't let dogs run away. He did good deeds. He cleaned up at home. And he didn't fight with his sister.

Well, let's not get too carried away.

Lexi was tutoring in the kitchen when I came home. I didn't recognize the girl next to her, but the girl looked frustrated. "Just try it again," said Lexi.

"It's too hard."

"No, it's not, Shelby," insisted Lexi, clearly annoyed.

"Yes, it is," Shelby whined.

"Fine, I'll just do it," Lexi said with a big grunt. She slid the girl's worksheet in front of her and wrote down an answer. No wonder kids liked having Lexi tutor them — she did their work for them! Lexi looked up at me and growled, "What are you looking at?"

"Nothing." I sneered right back at her. Maybe Little Miss

Perfect wasn't so perfect after all. "I'm surprised you have time to tutor, though." This was my chance for a little Lexi-bashing. "Have you made up the three tests you flunked last week?"

Shelby gasped and grabbed her worksheet back from Lexi.

"I did not flunk three tests," Lexi snarled, and snatched the paper back.

"Right, it was four," I said. "Silly me."

Shelby tried to grab her paper again, but Lexi lifted it out of her reach. "He's kidding," she hissed. "I've never flunked a test in my life."

Shelby didn't seem convinced. She reached for her homework, but Lexi threw daggers with her eyes. "Don't even think of touching this homework."

The girl put her hand down and sat rigid in her seat, quivering. "Okay," she squeaked. "You can have it."

Lexi was writing down answers as I left the room. I sort of felt a little bad about being mean to Lexi, but just a little. A very, very little.

Chapter 15

The next day I picked up Duchess, a small, light brown puggle with deep wrinkles in her forehead and drooping ears. Puggles are crosses between pugs and beagles, so they aren't big. She was a big-time sniffer, though. For some dogs, the world was nothing but a million wonderful scents. You would think a sidewalk would smell like sidewalk. But then, you're not a dog.

Smelling sorts of dogs like to smell everything, so it was hard to get Duchess going in the right direction. "C'mon, Duchess," I begged. "This way."

Duchess ignored me and smelled a lamppost.

"Duchess!" I wailed. "We've got money waiting."

Finally, we got to the street corner a few blocks away, although it took forever to get there. Thankfully, Fisher and about ten of his friends were still waiting. When they saw me, they cheered. I waved. If they each brought three dollars, and they each walked Duchess, well, I didn't have to do the math to know I'd be sitting on a big pile of money.

"One at a time," I shouted, handing the leash to some boy with snot all over his face. "You'll each get a turn."

I lay down against a tree. The day was warm. The shade felt good. "Walk for three minutes, and then pass Duchess to the next kid. Just don't let go of the leash," I muttered.

It was really peaceful under that tree. A bit too peaceful, it seems. Because the next thing I knew, someone was kicking my leg.

"What? Huh? Done already?" I mumbled, surprised. Standing above me was a lady, probably someone's mother, wearing an angry frown. She handed me Duchess's leash and shook her finger at me. Her face was flushed. "What do you think you're doing?" she screeched.

"Dog walking?" I said.

She yelled at me about stealing money from little kids. I tried to explain that I didn't steal anything — that it was all the law of supply and demand and they had a demand I was supplying. But the lady didn't want to hear any of it. She must not have studied economics in school. She made me return all the money to the kids and told me if she saw me charging kids again, she would call my parents.

And I couldn't let that happen. Mom would just say I was irresponsible. But I wasn't! I was trying!

It's just not as easy being responsible as you'd think.

And I needed to earn money quickly. I would have explained that to the woman, but she was already stomping away, leading the kids across the street. A bunch of them looked back at me, disappointed.

The lady was probably a cat person.

Back home, Lexi still tutored. I don't know how anyone could stand being around schoolwork for so many hours in the day. If it was me, my brain would have exploded. As I passed Lexi's room, her door opened and her friend Sophie walked out. They didn't notice me. I stopped in the hallway, my hand on my doorknob. I kept silent.

"Thanks, Lexi," said Sophie. "Sorry I can't pay you or anything."

"That's okay," said Lexi. "That's what friends are for."

"It's just that I'm saving my money to buy those shoes I was telling you about."

"Don't worry about it. Hannah isn't paying, either. Same time tomorrow?"

"You bet!"

As I turned my doorknob to go into my room, it squeaked just loudly enough for Lexi to notice. "What are you looking at, baby brother?" she snapped.

"I'm not a baby."

"Are you spying?" she snarled.

"I'm just standing here. It's a free country. And a free hallway. And apparently, free tutoring."

"It's none of your business what I'm doing," she barked.

"It's a shame people can't actually pay you." I removed a wad of cash from my pocket. "I wonder how much money I made today," I slowly counted out the bills. "Five dollars . . . ten dollars . . ."

"You don't know anything."

"I know we're getting a dog."

"We're getting a cat."

"A dog!"

Just then the doorbell rang. Lexi shook her head. "Whatever," she mumbled. She headed downstairs to answer the door.

"Another free lesson?" I called behind her. "Have fun! I'll be throwing all my money on my bed and rolling in it!"

"Baby brother!" yelled Lexi.

"I'm not a baby!"

Sticks and stones break bones, but names don't. I bet half of her customers weren't paying her. I couldn't help but smile. Her great tutoring plan wasn't so great after all. She should know nothing in life is free, especially pets.

She should create a glittery chart: how long it takes to earn five hundred dollars when you don't charge anyone money. The answer was forever. Even me, the non-math genius, knew that.

I went to my room, which was now my business office. All mega-companies need offices. I had my shoe box to keep my money in. I had my notebook to write down my appointments. I had three pencils to write with, and only two of them needed to be sharpened. I had a box of sandwich bags and brown paper bags to keep dog poop in. After all, You Oughta Call Otto's Dog Walking Service was about cleanliness. I had a calendar, although it was last year's. Still, a Tuesday is a Tuesday, right? It's not like the days change names every year.

I wrote down in my notebook:

"Pay Mom back for three pencils, sandwich bags, and paper bags: $8.00."

I threw the money I had collected that day on my bed. I greedily counted it. $22.52.

I thought I should have had more money, though. I had absolutely no idea where the fifty-two cents came from. I had been given a one-dollar tip by Mr. Roofus, but I must have given the wrong change back to Mrs. Greely. Or maybe I charged her the wrong amount. In fact, I think I had been making money mistakes every day.

I called Malcolm to tell him how well things were going, not including the math problems. Or my falling asleep. Or accidentally showing up late for every appointment that day. But it wasn't my fault my watch broke. Two weeks ago.

"My next appointment is at three thirty tomorrow," I told him, looking at a note I squinted to read. I was pretty sure it said three thirty. Yes, it said three thirty. Definitely.

Probably. I groaned.

"What was that?" asked Malcolm.

"Nothing," I said quickly. "Things couldn't be going better."

"It sounded like you groaned. Have you finished those math worksheets yet?"

"Almost," I answered, although I didn't remember getting any math worksheets. Still, *almost* can mean just about anything. When Mom asked if my room was clean, or if I was ready for bed, or if I was done with a chore, I'd just say, "Almost." Who could argue with that? "Things are perfect," I boasted to Malcolm, my fingers crossed.

I looked at another appointment scribble. The pencil tip had broken while I wrote down that address, so it was a little messy. I wasn't sure if I wrote 426 Pine Drive or 928 Pline Avenue. Pine. Pline. Those are stupid street names, anyway. They should name roads with names like the Amazing Otto Drive, the Unbelievably Awesome Otto Avenue, and the Super Terrific Otto Highway.

Maybe I could get paid for naming streets. I'd do it for a one-time fee of five hundred dollars. That would have been a pretty excellent deal if you asked me.

After I hung up with Malcolm, I stayed up kind of late looking over my notes and trying to read them. I was going to be on time tomorrow to my appointments.

I was going to try really hard to be extra responsible. After all, I was the new, responsible Otto.

Chapter 16

THURSDAY, MARCH 15—FRIDAY, MARCH 16
MONEY SAVED: $110.31

I sat in the school lunchroom with Malcolm, eating pizza. Unfortunately. School had the worst pizza in the history of pizza. It looked good. It smelled edible. I'd buy the pizza, thinking, *How bad could it really be?* And every time it still tasted spine-chillingly lousy. It didn't taste as bad as horseradish, but it was a close runner-up.

So I gnawed on the burnt, rubbery crust with tire-tasting sauce and runny, nauseating cheese, telling Malcolm my problems.

"No one wants every street named Otto," he said.

"Forget the street-naming part. That wasn't really the point." I tried to saw my teeth through the pizza crust. I think I might have chipped a tooth. I continued admitting my problems; it felt good to tell the truth. "I can't keep track of all my appointments. The You Oughta Call Otto Dog Walking Service is having growing pains, like the Incredible

Hulk." Malcolm stared at me, confused. "The Hulk is a dweeby science guy who turns into a giant monster but is still wearing the same pants. I mean, isn't your underwear riding up your butt when you're the Hulk? I know he's practically invulnerable and all, but that's got to hurt. I'd hate that."

"The Hulk doesn't get hurt when you shoot him with like a rocket missile, so I doubt tight underwear is going to be an issue in the pain department. But that's beside the point. You said last night everything was great —" began Malcolm.

"That was before I spent three hours trying to figure out what I wrote. Is there even a Pline Avenue?"

"I don't think so."

"That solves one problem," I said, relieved.

"You just need to be responsible," said Malcolm.

There was that word again. "I am!" I insisted.

"You need to keep a schedule. Organize your finances. It's not that hard."

"Easy for you to say." I pushed away my pizza. I needed my magician handsaw to finish it. "I can't track my appointments even if I had the rest of my natural born life to do it."

"Does that mean you can track it once you're a vampire?"

"I've been wondering the same thing." We both looked at each other for a few seconds thinking, but we didn't come up with an answer. "Anyway," I said. "Keeping track of time and money is not easy."

"For you," he scoffed.

"You could do better?"

"What do you think?"

Of course he could do better. Malcolm was practically a math genius. He won Mathlete-of-the-Year in fifth grade. He received a trophy and everything.

If you don't have Mathletics in your school, you probably don't know what I'm talking about. It's sort of like a spelling bee, but for math. You stand in a line and answer math questions. Everyone in school participates. I guess the math people were jealous of the spelling bee people, so they invented Mathletics. Other departments were thinking of doing the same thing. I had heard rumors that there might be a geography contest called Geographobia and a history contest called Historlympics. The school might also begin a sports contest with running and swimming and gymnastics, but I have no idea what they would call that.

"So?" I asked. "Are you going to help me get organized?" Malcolm laughed, but this was no laughing matter. "I'm serious! Are you?" Malcolm bit into his chocolate brownie dessert. He chewed very slowly. I stared at him, waiting for an answer. He continued to chew. "Hurry up and swallow already!"

Finally, he gulped down the food and said, "Maybe. How much are you going to pay me?"

"I'm saving for a dog!" I protested. "You're my best friend. You should pay me."

"Why would I pay you?"

"Fine, you shouldn't. Bad idea," I admitted. "But I can't pay you. I need to save every cent."

"You won't be making any cents unless you're organized."

That made sense. But giving Malcolm part of my hard-earned income would make it that much harder to win.

"Take it or leave it. I'm fine either way." Malcolm bit off another piece of brownie and sat back in his chair as if he didn't have a care in the world.

Remember when I mentioned the art of negotiating? You should always act like you don't care. That gives you the upper hand. I knew Malcolm was just pretending to be uninterested to get more money. But I was too smart for him. I could play that game, too. "I'll leave it, then," I said, shrugging.

"Great. Want to play soccer today?" suggested Malcolm.

"Wait," I said. "Hold on. We're still negotiating."

"You said you would leave it."

"That was negotiating." Obviously, Malcolm wasn't as shrewd a businessman as I thought he was. "How much do you want?"

"Twenty percent."

"Twenty percent?" I wailed. "I can't give you half of my money!"

"It's not half. It's one-fifth. You really are horrible at math, aren't you?"

Still, giving one-fifth of something is better than getting all of nothing. I held out my hand. "It's a deal." We shook on it. "But I'm in charge. This is my business. It's not 'You Oughta Call Otto and Malcolm's Dog Walking Service.' It's 'You Oughta Call Otto Dog Walking Service.'"

"I think 'You Oughta Call Otto the Mashed-Potato-Brain Bonehead' has a nice ring to it."

"Meat-loaf breath."

"Snot-nosed weasel-breeder."

"Cafeteria-pizza lover."

Malcolm stopped and looked at my mangled, half-chewed pizza slice. "Good one. I think you got me that time."

After lunch, we went to social studies class. I was just getting settled in my seat when Mrs. Swift cleared her throat. "Put your books away and take out your pencils," she announced, and began passing out tests.

"A surprise quiz?" I whispered to Malcolm.

Malcolm looked at me as if I was batty. "No surprise. Aren't you ready for it?"

"Almost." Now that I thought about it, I vaguely remembered something about a test today. On the Civil War, I think, maybe. Abraham Lincoln was our president back then. The North fought the South. The rest was a blur.

I don't think I did very well. But I couldn't flunk, or I'd be losing this war before I saved practically anything. Just when things were looking better, too.

"How'd you do?" Malcolm asked as we handed back our papers.

"Did Abraham Lincoln invent the top hat?" I asked. Malcolm shook his head. So I got at least one question wrong.

Malcolm came to my house after dinner. He brought an appointment book that his dad didn't need. He carefully rewrote the addresses and appointment times for every customer in it. When he couldn't read what I wrote, he found the person's phone number and called to confirm. He even changed a couple of appointments that I had accidentally double-booked.

The next best thing to being responsible by yourself is having someone being responsible for you.

So things were going great. Lexi's snarky smiles hadn't been seen in days, and my money was ready to grow to Incredible Hulk–like proportions, without the underwear issues. Nothing could go wrong now. That night as I sat at the table waiting for Mom to bring dinner over, I could practically smell my own dog leaping beside me, begging for scraps, eager to be a part of our family.

Although, actually that odor was on my hands from walking dogs all afternoon. It was a great smell, but I washed my hands before Mom yelled at me.

"Otto! Hang up your jacket!" Mom screamed from the hallway. She can always find something to yell at me about, though.

The next day, I showed up for all of my dog walking appointments on time, thanks to Malcolm's expert scheduling skills. But, to be perfectly honest, dog walking was still harder than I thought it would be. None of the dogs listened to me. They would go left when I wanted to go right, or backward when I wanted to go forward, or slow when I wanted to go fast. They were walking me more than I was walking them! One dog — Milo — didn't want to move at all and refused to budge even after I begged him for ten minutes.

I carried Milo most of the way. I figured that was okay because I promised to walk dogs, but I didn't promise that the dog would be the one doing the walking. Luckily, Milo was a toy poodle. That's a small dog.

You wouldn't think walking dogs would be tiring, but it is, even when you're not carrying them. My feet hurt. My legs ached. So I tried walking Grizella the American foxhound while riding my skateboard. Foxhounds are fast, so I thought it was a great idea, and pretty fun, too, except when she ran off the sidewalk and my skateboard skidded after her and I wiped out, which happened every seven seconds. "Don't turn!" Wipe out. "Hold on!" Wipe out. "No, not the tree!"

So I gave up that idea. I told Mom she needed to buy more bandages. I also asked if she minded if I walked dogs on her treadmill. I was with Chucky the Chihuahua at the time.

"Yes, I mind," she insisted.

"But it's not like you ever use it."

"I use it!"

But she really doesn't.

It might have been for the best, though. Chucky had serious bathroom issues. He must have peed every three minutes. It would have created a real mess on Mom's treadmill. To make things worse, he kept trying to pee on people. Maybe he thought people looked like fire hydrants. It's really awkward apologizing to a jogger for being peed on. It's even harder apologizing to one jogger while your dog is trying to pee on a different jogger at the same time.

I stopped, clutching Chucky's leash tightly. A cat crossed our path. A black cat, too. Chucky immediately growled and probably would have chased it if he hadn't been going to the bathroom. They say if a black cat crosses your path, bad things will happen. I hoped not. Five years ago I broke a mirror. I heard if you break a mirror you get seven years of bad luck. I still had two years to go. So if you added in the black cat, the odds were stacked against me.

"Come on, Chucky, let's jog!" I shouted after he had done his business. We broke into a light trot. I wanted to get away from that cat as fast as I could.

But maybe black cats were good luck. Because when I arrived home, I was almost barreled over by Kaitlin Singer stomping down the stairs. She was in Lexi's class and was in the school play the year before. She starred as Annie Oakley, and I'm pretty sure she was the best singer in school. But her voice sounded gruff and angry on the staircase, not melodic like it did on stage.

"Thanks a lot!" she howled, her face flushed red as if she had been crying.

"I'm sorry," stammered Lexi, hurrying down the steps after Kaitlin. Lexi's face looked red, too. Maybe they both had been crying. "I really am."

"Not everyone can be as smart as you," sniped Kaitlin. "I'm not stupid."

"I didn't say you were stupid. I said your answer was stupid."

"It's the same thing."

"Not technically. You just give stupid answers some-times," said Lexi. Kaitlin bolted to the doorway. "That's not what I meant." Kaitlin opened the door. "Are we still friends?"

"Never!" came the angry retort, followed by a door slam.

I stood there, just at the edge of the stairs. "What are you looking at?" Lexi demanded, her red, bloodshot eyes staring darts into me.

"It's looking like I'm getting a dog," I started to say, but I only got as far as "It's looking . . ." and then swallowed the rest. Lexi's face was so red, her eyes so filled with tears, that I didn't think I needed to say anything to make her feel any worse than she did.

Lexi sighed, dropped her shoulders, and walked past me and up to her room without saying a word.

There was nothing smug about her expression just then. I felt sorry for her. I truly did. But I shook off the feeling. You can't get soft when you're in the middle of a war.

Getting soft is how you lose. And I was going to win.

Dog walking went pretty well. With no school on Saturday, I had time for a little homework, too. Or I would have had time for a little homework if I hadn't fallen asleep. But I wasn't late for any appointments, at least.

True, dogs didn't actually walk in the direction I wanted them to, but only one dog peed on someone, so that wasn't so bad. Things were definitely looking up. Back home, Mom called an after-dinner meeting. Lexi and I cleared the dishes.

"How's it going?" Lexi asked me. We waited at the kitchen table while Mom finished putting the leftovers in the refrigerator.

"Awesomely great," I boasted.

Lexi nodded. "Me, too. I guess." But she didn't sound very convincing. "I just wish I had more time. I just wish the contest wasn't so short. But it's going by so quickly. I barely have time for anything."

"Yeah," I agreed, thinking of soccer and my schoolwork, and how I hadn't had time for either. "It'll be easier once the month is over."

"I hope so. It's like a school report. You think you have so much time to write it, and then all of a sudden it's two weeks later and the report is due!"

I nodded. "Yeah! Or when you're supposed to read a book and instead read comic books, and then the book report is due and you haven't even started it yet."

Lexi frowned. "I've never done that."

"Oh. Right." Figures.

"But I know what you mean," she added quickly. Mom closed the fridge. Lexi threw me a small smile. "Good luck."

"You, too." I returned her smile but caught myself, and changed it to a sneer. I wouldn't give Little Miss Perfect the satisfaction of a smile. This was not the time to start getting all mushy. Not now.

Mom joined us. She looked at Lexi and then at me. "So?" she asked, and took a deep breath. "How's the contest going?"

"Great," Lexi and I answered at the same time.

"Are you keeping up with school?"

"I am," Lexi and I said together.

"Otto? Is that true," Mom asked, slitting her eyes and staring at me, as if trying to read my mind. "You're all caught up with your homework?"

"Almost." I thought of the stack of homework I hadn't started. I knew my math worksheets were sloppy and half wrong. I had turned in my book report late — and I had only read half the book. Not that I would tell Mom any of this.

Mom nodded, apparently satisfied. "I'm proud of you, Otto. You're really being responsible."

I forced a broad smile, but it felt as fake as a movie set. "Just call me the New, Responsible Otto."

"I'd be even more impressed if you put your shoes and jacket away," Mom said, pointing to the pile in the middle of the hallway. My smile disappeared.

Then Mom turned to Lexi. "You're tutoring students all day long. But when do you have time for your own assignments?"

"Lots of time," she said. "I work on the bus and at lunch. And you know me. I always do great in school."

Lexi shifted on her seat uncomfortably. Her jeans might have been too tight, or perhaps she was stretching the truth a little. But I didn't say anything. I was doing some serious seat shuffling of my own.

"I'm not going to do much tutoring anymore anyway," Lexi said. "I have another idea. A better idea."

"What idea?" I asked, anxious. I sat at the edge of my seat. I didn't like the sound of that one bit. But Lexi didn't answer. Instead, she smirked. Which wasn't a good omen.

"I'm glad things are going so well," said Mom. "But if your schoolwork starts to suffer, either of you, this contest is over and we're not getting a pet. Don't forget."

"We know, Mom," I said. "Things couldn't be going better. In fact, things are perfect. Almost."

"The month is halfway over," said Mom. "How are you both doing on saving money? Otto? I know you had some struggles in the beginning." She didn't have to mention the Great Kitchen Calamity or the Awful Apple Atrocity, but I knew what she meant.

"I'm not having trouble anymore," I said, and at least this part was mostly true. "Dog walking not only pays well but it's great practice for owning a dog. You'll be really impressed by how well I can care for our dog when I win."

"I'm sure Otto will be a great help in taking care of Fluffernutter," said Lexi with a chuckle.

"We're getting a dog," I hissed.

"A cat, baby brother."

"I'm not a baby."

"You'll be crying like a baby when I win."

"Well, you smell like a baby who needs a diaper change! Stink bomb!"

"That's perfume!" she wailed.

"Stink bomb! Stink bomb!"

"Enough!" shouted Mom, resting her head on the table

and groaning. "Just remember to do your homework. And I hope you're both not working too hard."

"Not me!" I exclaimed.

But of course I was lying. We had a soccer game coming up in two weeks, and I bet Malcolm was practicing that very minute. Meanwhile, my feet ached from dog walking and I just wanted to go to bed.

But if Lexi had another great idea to earn money, whatever it was, I couldn't slow down. I could play soccer and do homework and take naps in a few weeks, after I had a dog. But right now I needed to win.

As soon as we were done talking, I called Malcolm and told him to come over for a business meeting. Whenever I thought of Lexi's smirks I grew more and more nervous. He was finishing dinner, but about fifteen minutes later he knocked on the door. We went up to my room.

"Lexi's up to something," I complained. "She has a great new idea. But I don't know what it is."

"Then how do you know it's great?"

"Because she smirked! We need to earn more money. Faster."

"And you have another horrible idea?" said Malcolm. His lack of faith in me was a bit depressing.

"No. I have an excellent idea." Even though the door was closed, I whispered just in case Lexi had her ear against the wall, snooping (although when I put my ear against the wall to snoop on her, I usually can't hear very much). "Lexi hates snakes," I said. When we were younger, I found a garter snake in the lawn and Lexi just freaked. "Let's fill her bed with snakes." I imagined Lexi turning back her covers and finding a dozen pythons wiggling around in there. I laughed out loud and rubbed my hands together.

"Um," said Malcolm. "Why do you want to put snakes in her bed?"

"Because Lexi hates them."

"But how will that help you earn more money?"

"How do I know? I don't care. I just like the idea of putting snakes in her bed. Do I need another reason?"

There was a pause before Malcolm spoke again. "Where would we find snakes?"

"I don't know." I admit, that was a problem. It would take days to capture enough of them to fill Lexi's bed, and I didn't have time to waste. Still, it was a good plan. Maybe someday. "Just look out for reptiles in general, okay?"

Malcolm rolled his eyes and shrugged.

I took the money I had earned that day out of my pocket and put it on my bed. Thanks to Malcolm I had earned thirty dollars on the nose — minus six dollars for Malcolm, plus four dollars in tips. Malcolm said I didn't have to share the tips, which was good because doing all the math was hard enough without trying to figure out his share of that, too.

"Thank you," he said, stuffing the money in his pocket.

I removed a shoe box — filled with my secret money stash — from the back of my closet. I shook it. Loose change jumped and clinked together. "I won't lose this war," I vowed. I wadded up my new bills and threw them in. Malcolm peeked inside.

"That's all the money you have?" he said.

"This is a lot," I insisted, but Malcolm didn't seem impressed. "Don't blame me. You're my accountant. You're supposed to make me rich."

Malcolm grabbed some of my bills and began straightening them, and then piling them into a neat stack. "You should open a bank account. Then you could earn interest and make even more money."

Anything that made me more money sounded good to me. "How much more? Can I double or triple what I have in two weeks?"

"Let's figure you'll earn one percent annually . . . compounded monthly . . . you might make about seven cents."

I grabbed the bills from Malcolm's hand, scrunched them into balls, and threw them back in the box. Straightening my bills had made my stash look even wimpier. "Seven cents?

No thanks. And I like my current money-keeping system, thank you."

"Scrunching up wads of money and keeping them in a shoe box is not much of a system," scoffed Malcolm.

"Maybe not, but it's my system, thank you. And money is worth the same no matter what shape it's in." As long as it's not ripped in half. Still, I didn't want to think about how much more I still had to earn. "Honestly — do you think we'll make it to five hundred dollars?" I bit my lip.

Malcolm hunched his shoulders. "I don't know. It'll be close. It's not impossible."

"Not impossible?" I punched my pillow. "That's not good enough. You should see how superior Lexi acts around me. I have to win!" I slammed my fist on my bed, but I missed and partially hit the bed frame. It really hurt. I stuck my knuckle in my mouth. My tongue helped it feel better. "We need to do something," I said after my finger stopped throbbing. My mind bubbled with possibilities. "We always have the snakes-in-bed thing."

"Forget the snakes." Malcolm leaned back on my bed. "Starting a business takes time."

"I don't have time!" I reminded him. "I need to up my game! Make my dog empire grow with leaps and bounds." My brain was churning. "I could break the world record for the most jelly beans eaten in one day, and then when I'm on TV I could tell everyone about my dog business." I love jelly beans, mostly. I mean, I don't love every flavor, like black licorice. No one likes black licorice, but you have to eat those, too, if you're going to break a jelly-bean-eating record. Which is why breaking that record is so impressive.

Malcolm just shook his head and said I needed to give it some thought. After he left, I paced in my room, thinking. I paced for so long that when I went to bed my legs felt like they were still tromping back and forth across the floor.

I sat up, opened my shoe box, and wadded my bills into tighter wads. It made me feel a little better.

ChaPTER 18

SUNDAY, MARCH 18
MONEY SAVED: $176.01

I dreamed I was trapped in a cage at the pet store, sur-rounded by other dogs. Thumper was there. So was Marta. I was tired and hungry, and my feet hurt. But when the pet store people came into the room, they weren't people at all. They were enormous pink cats standing on two legs, like people in cat suits. I yelled for them to let me out because I wasn't a dog but a kid, but the cats ignored me because they were having a giant cat party. They batted around huge balls of yarn and played pin-the-tail-on-the-sardine. There was a disco ball, too. It wasn't quite a nightmare, but it was close enough that when I woke up, I was shaking.

But it gave me a great idea. I called Malcolm immedi-ately. I think I woke him up.

"What? You woke me up," he complained. His voice croaked.

I told him all about my dream. "What do you think?"

"I think it's six o'clock in the morning," he mumbled.

"Actually, it's 5:58." I hadn't thought to look at the time before I called. "Sorry! But what if I threw a party?" Silence. "Hello? Malcolm? Hello?"

After a moment, Malcolm spoke again. "What? I fell asleep. Did you say a party? A party for what? A surprise party?" he mumbled.

Malcolm's mom threw a surprise party for his dad last year. Everyone hid. When his dad came home we all jumped out and screamed. Malcolm's father stepped backward, twisted his ankle, and knocked his head on a lamp. He spent the night in the hospital. Mom said Malcolm's mom would never throw a surprise party again for the rest of her natural born life.

"No, not a surprise party," I said. Malcolm exhaled. I think he was relieved. "Like an open house. So people can meet me and see how great I am with dogs, and I'll get all sorts of business."

"What does that have to do with your dream about cats playing with yarn?" asked Malcolm.

"Forget about the yarn part. The cats were having a party, with games and food. I could do the same thing."

After a short pause, Malcolm said, "But are you sure you could throw one? I mean, what would the dogs do?"

"They're dogs. How hard can it be? Besides, I'm going to throw the dog party to end all dog parties! We'll have dog treats and dog games. Dogs can make friends. Owners can mingle and talk about how wonderful my dog walking services are. I can even charge money."

"You can't charge money for a party."

"Sure I can. Last year I went to a block party. It was free, but they asked for donations. Mom gave a few dollars. People always toss money into jars or they feel guilty." I thought about my runaway dogs and other problems. I was quite an expert at feeling guilt. Plus, guilt is a great way to earn money. "I'll put out a giant jar with a donations sign. I'll drum up business and make a killing all in the same day. And I guarantee, people are going to be talking about Otto's Dog Party for years!"

Malcolm laughed. "I have to admit. The idea isn't terrible."

"I know, right? We'll throw the party this afternoon. You buy the dog treats and toys. You call our customers. You put up some signs. Let's go!" I pumped my fist. We were on!

"And what will *you* be doing?" asked Malcolm coolly.

"Resting. I'm the one that has to smile and play with the dogs. That's very strenuous work. And it's six o'clock in the morning. I really should go back to sleep."

"You woke *me* up," Malcolm said. "And how is smiling and playing such strenuous work?"

"I would tell you, but it would be too exhausting." I lay back on my bed and let out an audible yawn.

"I have a better idea. You buy the treats. You call the

customers. You put up the signs. I can't help. I'm going clothes shopping today with my mom."

I scoffed. "What's more important? Your wearing clothes, or my throwing a dog party?" He needed to adjust his priorities.

"The most important thing is me not getting into trouble, and I'll get in trouble if I tell Mom I'm not going shopping with her. I need to get a suit for my aunt Jewel's wedding."

"Isn't she the one that's been married six times?"

"Seven."

"You'd think you could skip a few." Malcolm's aunt Jewel kept getting married over and over again. If you ask me, she did it for the wedding presents. It seems like half the stuff we have at home Mom got as wedding presents, and she was married only once. After getting married seven times, Aunt Jewel must be a millionaire.

If I got married, I'd get way over five hundred dollars. Of course, that meant actually talking to a girl other than my sister. So I scratched that plan quickly.

It's a lot of work throwing a party, and I had all sorts of things I needed to do. I called my customers and invited them. I think I woke a bunch of them up even though I waited until after six thirty before I called. A few grumbled and one hung up. But I told everyone to invite their friends with dogs, and suggested they tell their friends with dogs to call *their* friends with dogs. Maybe, eventually, everyone in the world with dogs would show up.

Although I didn't think we could fit all those people in my front yard.

I promised treats, games, and the chance for their dogs to make new friends. Everyone would have the best time ever, hire me to walk their dogs, and I'd become a dog walking zillionaire.

Mom had bought some new printer toner. At first she was mad I used it all up last time, but then I showed her my notebook and told her I would pay her back as soon as the challenge was over. I told her I would even pay her back for her notepad, pencils, and more. I think she was impressed by how responsible I was being.

So I made some fliers and printed them. They were amazing.

IT'S DOG MEET DOG!

YOU AND YOUR CANINE ARE INVITED TO A DOG PARTY!

DOG TREATS! GAMES! GUARANTEED FUN!

PARTY STARTS AT 2:00 P.M.

SPONSORED BY THE YOU OUGHTA CALL OTTO DOG WALKING

SERVICE.

DONATIONS ARE WELCOME, PREFERABLY $5 BUT REALLY, IT'S

UP TO YOU. BUT DON'T BE CHEAP.

I printed two dozen fliers and put them up all over the block. Then I walked to the pet store for supplies. It opened at ten o'clock, so I had to wait until the doors opened. But as soon as they slid apart, I ran into the store. I figured I had a few extra minutes, so I could play with Thumper. But he was napping and I didn't want to wake him. Dogs, like people, must sleep in on Sundays.

There was one more empty cage, though: Thumper's sister, Marta, was gone. Probably adopted. If you jump around and bark, you get noticed, but if you're quiet, you get left behind. Lexi raised her hand in class and volunteered for things, so teachers loved her, while quiet Otto napping in the back of the class got overlooked. I guess that's not always bad, especially when you don't know the answers. But it was the point of the thing that mattered.

"Be yourself," I whispered to Thumper, although he couldn't hear me through the pane of glass, and because he was asleep. "And be glad you don't have to put up with your annoying sister anymore."

I ended up buying two bags of dog food and some dog toys for the party: a rubber duck, two fake bones, a Frisbee, and a little screaming monkey named Mr. Chatterbox. I hoped it was enough! I loved everything I got, except for maybe that screaming monkey. Frankly, Mr. Chatterbox sort of freaked me out. You squeezed his stomach and he went *eeep!* really, really loud. When I first pressed him, I must have jumped two feet in the air. I didn't really understand how a dog was supposed to play with a screaming monkey, but those dog-toy people must know what they're doing because they have college degrees in dog-toy making.

Besides, this wasn't a party for me. It was a party for dogs. I hoped they'd think Mr. Chatterbox was a riot.

Walking ten pounds of dog food home from downtown is not easy. I should have brought the red wagon. I stopped to rest a million times and almost gave up. It took nearly an hour to get home. But you can't say you'll have dog food and not serve dog food. That would be like having a surprise party and not yelling *surprise*. Except that would be a great way to avoid a concussion.

Once I was back at the house, I still had a lot to do if this was going to be the best dog party ever. I had to bring up our folding tables from the basement. We didn't have dog bowls, so I filled some of our nice soup bowls with water and some with dog treats.

Mom was at work, but she wouldn't have cared. Maybe.

I also made popcorn, since you can't have a party without popcorn. I scattered the toys around the front lawn, although I wished I had bought more. Five dog toys for an entire party didn't seem like enough, especially if I got a few hundred dogs. I figured every dog in the neighborhood would come. Who doesn't love a party?

I made small business cards with my name and phone number, printed them, and then cut them out with scissors. But most important, I put a giant bowl on a table and a sign that read, DONATIONS WELCOME $5 RECOMMENDED. I threw in a few dollars so the bowl didn't look so empty and to encourage guests. People never want to be the first ones to throw money into a bowl.

My giant donations container used to hold fish, but they all died a few years ago. Fishbowls get dirty. Eventually, streaks of green algae lined the sides of my bowl, and you could barely see the fish inside. Dad had to empty out the water, so he put all the fish in a bucket. But he didn't clean the bucket first and it had kitchen cleaner in it from the last time Mom mopped, and the fish died in like ten seconds. Lexi bawled for a week, even though they were just fish and she never even looked at them, ever. Fish don't do a whole lot.

I paced nervously in front of the yard. Where were all the dogs? It was already 2:01 and no one was at my party yet. This was a disaster.

"What are you doing?" asked Lexi, sticking her head out the door.

"Throwing a dog party. What do you think?"

"I think you're pacing on our lawn. I don't see dogs."

"They're coming," I said. "Any moment now."

Lexi scanned the street. "Still don't see anyone." She scanned the street again. "Still no one."

"They'll be here. It takes money to make money."

"It takes brain cells to have a brain."

"Then too bad you don't have any!"

She shook her head, chuckled, and went inside. Just in time, too. She wasn't going to ruin this party like she ruins everything else. A few minutes later the first guest trotted up — a small, bald guy wearing thick glasses, with a large black Doberman.

"Welcome to the dog party!" I exclaimed with my biggest smile. "You're the first ones, but we're expecting two hundred dogs!"

"Two hundred?" the man blubbered. He had some sort of tic and his eyes kept blinking, but not at the same time. It was sort of freaky. "Maybe we should go. Dodger doesn't like big crowds." He snuck a nervous peek at the Doberman.

"Well, maybe not two hundred," I assured him. "Your dog will be fine." I couldn't lose my only guest. I pointed to the former fishbowl. "It's free, but donations are welcome." Dodger's owner took out a dollar bill. "Five dollars is better," I suggested. The guy frowned but coughed up the dough. "I also walk dogs, you know!" I handed him one of my business cards. "I'm not only great with dogs, but I'm ultra-responsible," I said.

The man looked at my card and nodded. "We could use a dog walker," he said.

Bingo! Meanwhile, another party guest jogged up the sidewalk, a leash in her hands. She had a golden retriever that looked a lot like Alfalfa. I rushed over.

"Welcome to the dog party. Five dollars, please."

"I thought it was free?" she asked.

"Donations are encouraged," I said, and pointed to the jar. She paid up. I was going to earn a bundle from this party.

I made a list in my head of other things I could collect donations for:

The Help, I'm Stuck Living with Lexi Fund
The Help Me Find the Circus So I Can Sell Lexi Charity
The Help Me Buy Snakes to Put into Lexi's Bed
   Foundation

The options were endless. Too bad I didn't have more fishbowls. If I did, I bet I could have earned five hundred dollars by dinnertime.

I handed the jogger my card. "And I'm the best dog walker in town. Just ask anyone! Well, not anyone," I added softly.

"Let's get a treat, Precious," said the woman to her golden retriever, leading her to one of the food bowls. But the Doberman decided he wanted that bowl at the same time. He growled and bared his teeth as Precious got close.

"Dodger! No!" said the short, bald guy, tugging on Dodger's leash. The guy's eyes blinked randomly.

"Back, Precious, back!" said the woman jogger to her golden retriever. Precious was tough, though. She was only half the size of Dodger, but she stood her ground. Still, things didn't look good.

"No problem," I assured them. "I'm a professional dog walker, after all." This was just the sort of thing that would impress future clients. I bent down and patted the Doberman's back. "It's okay, boy." Dodger snapped at me, and then at Precious. "You're supposed to have fun at a party!" Dodger snapped at me again. I took a few steps back. There are some things even professional dog walkers can't fix.

But I couldn't stay to watch, because more dogs and their owners approached. This was going great, except for the potential dogfight about to break out.

"Five dollars, please!" I pointed to the jar. The owners looked puzzled. "It's a donation," I explained. "But everyone's giving."

Meanwhile, Dodger and Precious still barked at each other, but more angrily than before. Two of the new dogs barked, and another dog began to cower. A woman with a poodle walked up the sidewalk, but she saw all the growling and turned around. I bent down and whispered calming words to a barking boxer that had just come up the path, but it was like the dogs weren't even listening. Which I guess shouldn't have surprised me. Then more dogs came up the sidewalk. "Donation jar!" I shouted.

I'm not sure when Buttercup showed up, but I couldn't miss her yapping. *Yap*, jump. *Yap*, jump. Her squealing riled up a German shepherd that I hadn't noticed, which began barking back. I must have had a dozen dogs at the party. Ten of them growled, one yapped, and one cowered behind its owner's legs.

"We have dog toys," I shouted, hoping some of the dogs might get distracted and settle down.

Then a brown-and-black dachshund — I think its name was Oscar but I'm not sure about that — found Mr. Chatterbox. I heard the screaming monkey before I saw it. The loud *eeep!* came from behind where Dodger and Precious snapped, their owners still struggling to hold them back. As soon as the monkey made a noise, however, the two dogs stopped. They stared at the monkey, their eyes fixated on the toy.

But it wasn't just them. All the dogs stopped and stared, except for Buttercup, who continued yapping and leaping. I have to hand it to those dog-toy people. I guess they earn those diplomas. Dogs love Mr. Chatterbox.

But the quiet felt even scarier than the growling. The air was thick with tension. Something bad was going to happen. I took two steps toward my house.

Dodger and Precious continued staring at Oscar and Mr. Chatterbox. Their eyes growing wider, their mouths expanding. Drool dripped off Dodger's fangs. All the dogs except Buttercup gaped: eleven dogs, one toy. Oscar dropped the toy and stepped back. I think he realized he was in deep trouble. When the monkey hit the ground, it made a soft *eeep*.

That did it. Dodger rushed forward. So did Precious. So did the poodle, the boxer, and most of the other dogs. Some of the owners were so surprised they released their leashes. Suddenly, we had half a dozen runaway dogs. But they weren't running away. They were headed straight for Mr. Chatterbox.

I guess this is how people must act the day after Thanksgiving, when they go to all those early Christmas sales and start fighting over the last mega-robot toy. Six dogs pounced on poor Mr. Chatterbox at pretty much the exact same moment. Even Buttercup got in on the action as poor Mrs. Linkletter shrieked, "*Come back to Mama!*"

The poor stuffed monkey's screams were now screams of agony, as pieces of face, fur, and arms were ripped to shreds by a horde of frenzied dogs. Two dogs played tug-of-war with a leg. Another dog ate Mr. Chatterbox's head and then threw it up.

I didn't want to watch, but it was like a traffic accident. I sort of had to look, even though it was horrible.

Owners grabbed leashes and desperately yanked their pets away from the melee. Dodger's owner's eyes were blinking a hundred times a second as he finally pulled his Doberman away. With no toy left to rip apart, the dogs lost interest.

Luckily, no one was injured. Not including Mr. Chatterbox, of course. He had basically disintegrated into a thousand tiny pieces.

"Who wants to play dog games?" I asked, waving the Frisbee.

Apparently, no one. That was the end of the party. The owners marched off with their dogs, angry, as if it was all my fault. "You oughta call Otto!" I said, trying to pass out my business cards, but no one wanted anything to do with them, or me. Dodger's owner even tossed my card back at me!

Mrs. Linkletter walked away angry, too, and I'm pretty sure Buttercup stopped yapping just long enough to snarl at me. But how was I supposed to know that Mr. Chatterbox would be so popular?

Just as bad, almost everyone grabbed their money back from the jar. Two of Mom's soup bowls had broken in half, and the rest were covered in dog spit. She was going to kill me. *And* I'd have to add the cost of replacing them in my notepad. I sat on my front lawn, my head in my hands, a piece of Mr. Chatterbox's arm on the ground next to me.

I looked up at the house. Lexi watched from her bedroom window. When she spotted me noticing her, she closed the blinds. But not before I saw what I think was a smirk on her lips.

I picked up the bowls and started to clean up. The war would end in less than two weeks, and my brilliant ideas were causing more harm than good. Meanwhile, Lexi was probably going online right this very moment to pick out cat clothes to buy for Fluffernutter.

CHAPTER 19

My list of things I owed Mom was getting pretty long, so I didn't want to use any more of her printer toner unless I really, really had to. Luckily, students can use the color printer in the main office at school for free. You're only supposed to print a single copy of something, but no one watches you. About a month ago, I made a hundred copies of a picture instead of one copy, just by accidentally pressing a couple of zeros. So when I printed my dog walking fliers, no one noticed I made thirty-six copies. It also helped that I made copies at the end of the day when everyone just wanted to go home.

I think those office people got more excited about the school bell than us kids did.

Armed with my pile of color fliers, I went to get my backpack out of my locker. Like always, I tried to avoid staring at those stupid Lexi tutoring signs on the walls. But I still peeked, just a little. And I immediately noticed something different about them. I stopped, frozen. It was a horrifying sight, a vision I thought might creep into my brain and give me spine-chilling nightmares for weeks on end.

I stared at a wall of glitter. But they weren't Lexi's tutoring signs on the walls. These were new. A dozen giant poster boards lined the hallway, each screaming the message: VOTE FOR SMOTE! CARLY SMOTE FOR STUDENT BODY PRESIDENT. I didn't have anything against Carly. I knew who she was, sort of. But I stared at the caked-on glitter, the fancy lettering, the immaculately detailed picture of a goat. DON'T BE A GOAT, VOTE FOR SMOTE. That didn't make a whole lot of sense, but the goat picture was pretty impressive.

There was only one person who could have made these posters.

Lexi.

As I plodded down the hall, gasping, gaping at every sign, I heard voices from around the corner. I recognized the evil voice of Lexi. I stopped, listening. I wasn't eavesdropping, though. It's never okay to eavesdrop. I was spying. There's a big difference.

"The signs are really good," said a boy's voice.

"Thanks," answered Lexi. "They were a lot of work."

"How much is she paying you?"

"I shouldn't say."

"I'll double it. I need signs like those."

"I don't know. I promised Carly I'd help her out," said Lexi.

"I'll triple the price!"

"You have yourself a deal."

As the sounds of their footsteps faded away, I stood in my spot, fuming. Sign making! That must have been the new moneymaking idea Lexi mentioned at dinner.

I looked down at my thirty-six pathetic, copy-paper-sized fliers. I had a little time before my first dog walking appointment. I hurried back to the office to make more copies.

Malcolm stopped over at my house in between dog walking jobs. He'd bragged at lunch about his soccer juggling, and I'd bet him ten dollars I could beat him blindfolded. I was the soccer star, not him. And I could use all the extra cash I could get.

I was in a good mood despite the Dog Party Debacle, because we got our Civil War tests back and I got a D. Which means I didn't flunk! But after class Mrs. Swift asked me if anything was wrong and said I needed to bring my grades up or she would call my mother.

Calling Mom would not be good. I assured my teacher everything was perfect, and I'd do better next time. And was she absolutely, unquestionably sure Abraham Lincoln *didn't* live at the Gettysburg Address?

She said she was absolutely sure.

"Watch this fancy dribbling," I boomed to Malcolm in my backyard. I bounced the ball on my left knee, my right knee, and then it hit my chin and bounced away.

"Impressive," jeered Malcolm. He then kneed the ball back and forth, and from one foot to the other. He juggled. And juggled. And juggled. Up and down and over and back. "You owe me ten dollars."

I shook my head. "I said I could beat you blindfolded. But we don't have a blindfold, so I guess we'll never know." Saved by a technicality.

"You could close your eyes."

"Not the same thing at all."

Malcolm still juggled. He kicked it off his foot and then back to his knee, and then performed a nice fake wave with one foot before spinning it up with the other. I never should have taught him that move.

"Show-off," I spat. "I can beat you with two legs tied behind my back, you know," I crowed, trying to act confident. But I didn't feel confident at all.

"How is that even possible?" he asked. "Really. Both your legs tied behind you? What would you kick with?"

"Okay, well, maybe not both legs, then," I admitted. "One leg. I can beat you with one leg tied behind my back."

"Still impossible. What are you going to stand on when you kick?"

"Well, I can still beat you with nothing tied."

"I think your brain is tied," laughed Malcolm. This entire time he still juggled. The ball never hit the ground, and it was really annoying.

I knew it wasn't his fault he was better than me at everything these days. Well, maybe it *was* his fault. He could miss a few soccer kicks at practice to make me feel better. Or at least one. He didn't have to be so much of a show-off. And maybe if he helped me more, I'd have more money and I wouldn't be almost flunking classes.

I walked over and shoved him. The ball bounced away.

"What did you do that for?"

I shrugged. "I have to go inside and get ready for my next appointment."

Malcolm checked his watch. "We have a minute."

"I'm in charge and I say we don't."

"You're in charge of time?" asked Malcolm. "Like Father Time?"

"Exactly," I grunted. "I am the lord and master of all that is time related. And all things dog-walking related, too. Don't forget that. My business. You just work for me."

Malcolm picked up the ball. "You're getting a little bossy," he huffed as he followed me inside my house.

"I am the boss," I snapped. "So what else would I be?"

"I don't know. Nice?"

"Bosses aren't nice," I retorted. "Don't you watch TV? Bakery bosses. Dance bosses. Restaurant bosses. All mean. That's the way things get done!"

I stomped upstairs to my room and Malcolm followed. I grabbed the stack of fliers from school and shoved them at him. "Now, I need you to go around town and post these signs up." After the Dog Party Debacle, I needed more customers. I spoke in my best boss voice: "And get a move on it."

"I'm the organizer and money guy, not the sign taper." Malcolm folded his arms and didn't reach for my fliers.

"You're what I say you are. I'm in charge, remember?" I thrust the stack at him again, but he didn't grab it.

"You could at least say *please*!"

"Bosses never say *please* or *thank you*. They just say *do this* and *you're fired*." I thought Malcolm knew a lot about economics, but apparently he didn't know how business worked at all. "Or do you want to just go around showing off your soccer moves instead?" I barked.

"What does that mean?"

"You know," I hissed.

"Well, I'm not putting up your stupid signs."

"They are not stupid. What does this say?" I demanded. I jabbed the paper with my finger.

Malcolm squinted and read: "'I'll walk your dog and clean up, too. Even if he goes number two.'"

Pretty good, huh? But that's not what I was pointing to. "No. Below it," I snarled.

Malcolm looked more closely at my flier. "'You Oughta Call Otto's Dog Walking Service.'"

"Exactly. Otto. Me. Your name is not here." I jabbed the page, harder. "We talked about this. This is *my* business. What I say goes. Does it say, 'You Oughta Call Otto and his Stupid and Lame Assistant Malcolm's Dog Walking Service'? No, it doesn't."

"I don't care. I'm still not putting up signs." He crossed his arms. "And *you're* stupid and lame."

"You're a mold-faced brain drain," I replied, crossing my arms, too. Only I crossed mine a little higher.

"You're an IQ-challenged wombat."

"You're an empty-headed vacuum head."

"You're a mulch-breathing hamster-eating vomit brain swimming in stink!" You know the worst part of the insult? He didn't even smile when he said it.

"Well, s-so are you!" I sputtered.

"You know what? I don't need your stupid twenty percent. Just forget it. I quit." Malcolm wheeled around and headed toward the door.

"You can't quit. You're fired!" I yelled back. "I'd rather keep your half of the money, anyway."

"Twenty percent is not half!" hollered Malcolm as he reached the front door.

"Says you!"

"No, says the math world!" Malcolm slammed the door behind him.

Who needed a show-off like him anyway? All I needed was a dog. I didn't want any help, or even a stupid best friend. A dog was man's best friend. When I won this challenge I'd have my own best friend jumping and licking me. Dogs don't insult you. And they never, ever, ever quit their jobs.

"You're late," barked Coach Drago, looking at his watch. It wasn't really my fault. Mitzi the German shepherd just wouldn't go to the bathroom. Some of these dogs are way too choosy about where they poop. You'd think every swatch of lawn was the same. Then when Mitzi finally squatted, I realized I had left my plastic clean-up baggies at home, so we had to run away really fast. No one saw us, but some poor family was going to find a surprise on their lawn.

I felt a little bad, but what was I supposed to do — put it in my pocket?

But at least I showed up to practice. Coach should have been happy to see me, but he didn't act like it.

"I've been busy," I explained.

"You need to be here. You need to be on time. If you're not committed to this team, I'll play kids who are."

"Yes, Coach. I know, Coach," I said, frowning so he knew I was serious. "But I have a good reason. Do you like dogs or cats?"

"Cats. Why?"

"Never mind."

Malcolm frowned at me, but I returned it with an even nastier frown of my own. I'd show him my awesome soccer talents. He'd see I wasn't the boss of him just in the business world, but on the playing field, too. It was about time I put him in his place.

I joined the line for shooting drills. The team was already practicing them. It was pretty simple: take a pass, one dribble, and shoot.

"Otto! What are you doing!" yelled Coach. My shot bounced meekly to the left, about ten feet away from the goal.

"Sorry," I mumbled.

"The bench needs more benchwarmers."

"Yes, Coach. Sorry, Coach."

Malcolm was next, and he buried his shot into the top corner of the net. It even had a slight bend. Where did that come from?

"That's how it's done," yelled Coach Drago, clapping. "Nice shot." Eric Lansing, our midfielder, then ran up, dribbled, and kicked a laser into the back of the net. "Beautiful kick!" shouted our coach.

I stood in line waiting for my next turn. Malcolm was in back of me. "You don't think Coach would really bench me, do you?" I grumbled.

"I think Coach should play the guys who show up to practice on time." He turned his back to talk to Kyle Krovitch, completely ignoring me.

Soon it was my turn again. I concentrated as hard as I could. I stared laser beams into that ball. Then I stutter-stepped and kicked more mightily than anyone had ever kicked a ball before in the world's history of soccer kicking. I imagined the ball ripping through the net, leaving Malcolm's and Coach Drago's mouths open in awed wonder.

I missed the ball completely. I waved my arms like a chicken, a particularly clumsy chicken, before toppling over and landing on my butt.

Coach Drago didn't say anything, but he wasn't smiling, either. I didn't even look at Malcolm. I'm pretty that sure he, on the other hand, smiled broadly.

I sat at the kitchen table after dinner. Lexi was in her room, which is where she had been all afternoon, with her door closed. She was probably making signs that very moment.

The downstairs was dark except for the light over my head, shining down on the math worksheets in front of me. I needed to catch up on my schoolwork, but my eyes were heavy and the numbers on the pages kept blurring together. Maybe if I had listened in class I would know what I was supposed to do, but I found the day went by much faster if I doodled dog pictures. I was getting pretty good at them. If we had a dog doodling test at school, I'd probably get an A.

But here, at the kitchen table, I just wanted to sleep. Dog walking. Soccer practice. It was all exhausting.

I stood up, opened the refrigerator, and took out a bottle of horseradish. I dipped my finger in the jar, and then plunged it in my mouth.

Every nerve in my body jumped up in shocked disgust as the horror of spice-filled yuckiness seeped through my throat. I grabbed a glass and filled it with water. But even after gulping it down, and a second glass, too, the terrible taste still coated my tongue in such sheer, bold thickness that I worried the pungent horseradish flavor might last forever.

But it did wake me up. Mission accomplished.

Mom drinks coffee to wake herself up, but I should tell her about the horseradish trick.

I finished one side of the first math worksheet, although I'm not sure the answers were exactly right. I didn't completely understand this radius concept. But at least there were answers on the page.

I turned the worksheet over to begin side two. I didn't want to think about how many more worksheets I still had to get through tonight. And I still needed to do my assigned reading in language arts.

The horseradish taste faded away after a few minutes, and so did my wakefulness.

I don't remember my dream exactly, but I do remember a cat yelling at me about being late, and Coach Drago purring on my lap. Lexi was laughing, and Malcolm was juggling jars of horseradish with his feet. I'm unsure how long I slept, but when I awoke, I found my head lying on the worksheet and the rest of the house fast asleep. I sighed and took a complete stab in the dark as to the area of a circle.

Lexi didn't have to worry about her grades; that always came easy for her. She didn't face the problems I did. She was good at *everything*. It wasn't fair.

I blame Dad. *And* Mom.

But that was just another reason why it was crucial that I won this war. I needed to show her, and Mom, and I guess even myself, that I was better than Lexi at something important.

I sighed and turned my attention once again to the worksheets, trying to remember what the difference was between a circumference and a diameter. I had no idea. Maybe I would remember after I took another nap on the kitchen table. A big yawn crept out of my mouth.

As my eyes closed, I noticed my soccer cleats in the middle of the floor. I needed to put them away. As soon as I woke up.

Chapter 20

TUESDAY, MARCH 20—WEDNESDAY, MARCH 21
MONEY SAVED: $176.77

At least with Malcolm out of the picture, I kept every penny I earned. Who needed him anyway?

I could do just fine without him, if only I could read my handwriting. I really needed to work on my penmanship. I went to the wrong houses. I accidentally showed up at the wrong times.

I even charged people the wrong amounts of money.

The worst money exchange happened when I dropped off Chucky the Chihuahua.

"That's six dollars, please," I said to Ms. Greenleaf.

"I have a ten," she said, dipping into her purse. "Do you have change?"

I counted out four singles. "Here you go."

"Wait. Here's a twenty."

"No problem." I counted out five more singles and a five.

"I don't want all these singles." She handed five of them back to me. "Can I have another five-dollar bill?"

"Sure." I gave her one.

"Oh, look. I have a ten. Can I get change for it?"

I handed her two five-dollar bills.

She handed me one of the bills back. "I'll take ones, please."

I counted out five ones.

"And can I have my twenty-dollar bill back?"

"Sure." I handed her the twenty and she handed me a stack of singles and fives.

"And do you have change for the twenty?"

I sighed but gave her some fives and some singles back.

This went on for a while. When I got home I realized that somehow I paid *her* five dollars.

I also walked a pig. On the phone, I thought Mrs. Ryan said she needed me to walk a *pug*. Hamlet the potbellied pig was small, fat, and slow. Plus, he snorted constantly and did not want to move. Mrs. Ryan told me he would chase after food, so I had to hold some corn in my hand and have him run after me. I was scared to death of banging into something and then having Hamlet jump on top of me and eat all the corn. Then I'd never get him home again. I'd probably never get him off me, either.

But it went all right, I guess. We made it around the entire block. But I wasn't planning on walking any more pigs.

After that, I rode my bike up to Grand River Avenue, my fliers tucked under my arm. I put them on lampposts and car windshields and walls and anywhere else I could think of. I'd make You Oughta Call Otto's Dog Walking Service a household name.

Dog walking. Not pig walking.

But I hadn't been the only one putting up signs. Lexi had been busy. Again. Unfortunately for me.

Everywhere I turned, I saw signs that made me feel more and more depressed. In the window of the hair salon was a bright pink poster that read, HAIR'S LOOKING AT YOU, KID! but with Lexi's unmistakable glitter style. When I went to get a better look, my fears were confirmed. In small print at the bottom were the words, SIGNS BY LEXI.

I felt dizzy and had to sit down on the sidewalk for a moment.

I noticed other signs, too. The hardware store window featured a poster with a picture of a hammer and the words IT'S HAMMER TIME AT LOUIE'S HARDWARE HOUSE! On the bottom were those three dreadful words that felt like someone had pummeled me in the stomach with a watermelon: SIGNS BY LEXI.

I put some of my signs up, but my heart wasn't in it. My signs seemed so small and uninteresting compared to Lexi's glitter monstrosities.

Had she earned five hundred dollars for a pet? Was she close? I was so far away from earning that much. After doing horrible at school, in soccer, and losing my best friend — what if I lost the Pet War, too?

The thought was too horrible to even imagine.

Chapter 21

Toby looked a lot like his owner, Mr. Jacoby. They both had stubby noses, wide heads, and big jowls. They both made an odd ticking sound in their throats, too. Dogs often take after their owners, though. Napoleon the Scottish terrier had a mustache just like Mr. Spanolli. Dakota the Afghan hound could've been Ms. Preston's long-lost sister, if Ms. Preston was a dog.

Which means my dog would be the best and handsomest dog ever.

I bet my dog would even play soccer.

Toby was a bulldog with a major slobbering issue. I'm not sure if Mr. Jacoby slobbered, too. He probably did. Toby was like a leaky faucet. Occasionally he'd shake his head and spray saliva everywhere in big, thick, sticky droplets. So I had to be on my toes to avoid them.

He walked faster than you'd think he could. I tried to pull the leash back, but I was no match for him. It was either keep up or be dragged. Whenever I told him to slow down, he'd cock his head to one side as if asking, "Really? You can't keep up? Are you kidding me? Look how short my legs are!"

Still, he was a great dog — energetic, fun, friendly. Really, those might be the best sorts of dogs of them all, if you thought about it. When I yelled at him, he didn't seem to mind. He didn't listen, either, but you can't have everything.

Mr. Jacoby had warned me not to feed Toby anything. I guess he got sick easily. But we were here to walk, not eat, so I didn't worry about it.

Just thinking about food made me hungry, though. It was really tiring jogging for so long. So when I passed the Wow Cow Ice Cream Parlor, and saw a kid about my age walking out the door with a vanilla ice-cream cone, my stomach started growling.

Ice cream is practically the best food ever made.

I had money in my pocket. I needed to save every penny, but two dollars wouldn't be the end of the world. Every now and then you have to treat yourself, right?

Too bad there was a sign on the ice-cream shop door that said, NO DOGS ALLOWED. But at least there wasn't any glitter on the sign.

I didn't know the kid with the ice-cream cone, but he looked honest enough. He was tall with freckles, and I didn't see any scars. You should never trust people with scars.

And he was eating vanilla ice cream. Bad people didn't eat vanilla.

"Hey," I said with a friendly wave. "Could you hold my dog while I grab a cone? It'll just be a minute."

The boy sniffed. "I'll do it for a dollar."

"It'll just be a few seconds," I replied.

"A dollar," he repeated, spitting.

He was a tough negotiator. But it was only a buck, and I really wanted the ice cream, so I handed him the leash.

"Pay in advance," he demanded, palm out.

I grumbled, but I fished a buck from my pocket and handed it over. "Hold it tight, okay?"

"Yeah, yeah," the kid said, shaking his head. "I know how to hold a leash."

As I walked away, I thought about telling the kid what Mr. Jacoby said about Toby's delicate stomach and all.

Nah. What sort of irresponsible kid would feed someone's dog ice cream? I dashed inside.

There were practically a million flavors to choose from. I couldn't decide, so I asked if I could taste a dozen of them, including pistachio almond and cherries jubilee. I finally settled on tin roof: vanilla ice cream, chocolate-covered peanuts, and fudge ripple. It's practically heaven on a cone.

"Keep the change." I slipped the guy behind the counter

two bucks. The price was $1.98. I felt generous. Ice cream will do that to you.

When I stepped back outside, the freckled kid and Toby were still there. They hadn't moved. Except Toby was the one with the ice-cream cone now. The boy laughed while Toby ate it up. Toby loved it, too. I thought it was pretty funny until I remembered Toby's eating problems.

Toby took a step back. The cone was all eaten. He didn't look very happy.

"What's wrong with your dog?" asked the freckled kid.

"How much did you give him?" I asked.

The kid shrugged. "All of it."

Then Toby vomited all over the sidewalk and part of my shoe.

"He has a weak stomach," I explained meekly.

I tossed my own cone away. The smell of vomit will kill your appetite. Toby threw up again.

"Are you okay, boy?" I asked him.

In response, Toby belched.

We walked home pretty slowly after that. Toby didn't feel like jogging anymore. I wasn't in a hurry to get back, either. I was going to have a hard time looking Mr. Jacoby in the eye.

"What's wrong?" asked Mr. Jacoby when we got back. Toby looked a little green. Then he burped again.

"Your dog loves ice cream," I stammered, handing him Toby's leash and wiping the back of my shoe on his patio step.

I didn't get a tip.

My appointments were messed up again. I had an appointment with a new dog, Gaga. I showed up at exactly five o'clock. I was pretty proud that I was on time for once.

"I needed you at four o'clock," fumed Mrs. Polansky. She shot me a frosty stare under slanted eyebrows. She held Gaga, a small, fuzzy white Havanese, in her arms. Normally, they're cute, happy dogs. But Gaga shared the same evil stare as her owner. She even had the same eyebrows. But then again, dogs do look like their owners.

"I thought it was now," I blurted out.

"Now is not four o'clock."

"Maybe you forgot to set your clocks ahead during daylight savings time a few months ago. Or is it moved them back? I always get confused."

She closed the door on me, so I guess that wasn't it.

But at least it meant I wouldn't be too late for the five fifteen appointment that I'd made and had misread. It was with Buttercup, and she still annoyingly yapped and jumped the entire walk. After the Dog Party Debacle, I was surprised Mrs. Linkletter even called me. I guess she recognized my dog walking excellence, even though she claimed I was the cheapest dog walker around and better than nothing.

But I'd show her! I walked Buttercup extra long to impress her. Unfortunately that meant I missed my next appointment, which I remembered about two hours after it was scheduled. I called to apologize, but the owner hung up on me. I guess I can't blame him, though.

The new, responsible Otto wasn't feeling very responsible.

My fliers kept getting new customers, but many only used me once and never again. They said they needed someone who was more dependable. I was dependable, I told them. I just wasn't particularly good with addresses or time or money. But I was trying. That had to count for something. Right?

I needed Malcolm. Malcolm knew exactly how much to charge. He told me exactly where to go and when.

That's a funny thing about being a boss. It doesn't do any good if you have no one to boss. But if you boss people too much, then they won't stick around to be bossed anymore. No wonder bosses make so much money. They need to get paid just to keep track of the whole thing.

And I'd never tell Malcolm this, but I sort of missed hanging out with him.

So I knocked on Malcolm's door after dinner. His mom answered and told me Malcolm was up in his room. I ran upstairs. He was doing homework. I was so far behind in my homework, I hated to even think about doing my own. So I tried not to. It was just depressing.

"What do you want?" Malcolm snarled, looking up from his desk.

"Whatcha doing?" I asked with a warm, casual smile, as if nothing had happened between us.

"Homework. What do you think?" he replied.

I stared at him for a moment, and he glared back.

"Look. I'm sorry," I muttered softly, breaking the quiet.

"What?" asked Malcolm. "You'll need to speak louder."

"Sorry," I muttered again.

"What?"

"I'm sorry!" I yelled. "I know I was too bossy."

"You weren't bossy. You were an inconsiderate, egomaniacal, narcissistic turd brain."

"I don't know what half those words mean," I admitted. "But I probably was."

"Say them out loud: 'I was an inconsiderate, egomaniacal, narcissistic turd brain.'"

I sighed. "I was an inconsiderate, ego-something, something turd brain."

"Close enough." Malcolm smiled, and his smile was the best thing that had happened to me in days.

I plopped down on his bed, relieved. "You could rejoin the business, if you want."

"No thanks."

"You could make lots of money."

"No thanks."

I decided to throw pride out the window. I sat up and clasped my hands together. "Please? I can't do this alone. Everything is messed up. I need you to balance my books. Make my appointments. Tell me how much to charge. I'm a great dog walker. Well, maybe not great. But with my dog walking and your business savvy, there will be no stopping us. Maybe."

Malcolm looked at me. His mouth curved from a smile, down to a frown, and then back up to a smile again. "Fine. Okay. I'm in. But I want twenty-five percent of the profits this time."

"But that's more than half!" I shouted.

"No. It's not."

"Fine," I relented. We shook on it. But I would have given him more than half the money to be my friend again. Not that I would have told him that. I know dogs are a man's best friend, but everyone needs a human best friend, too. Having both is best of all.

CHAPTER 22

Mom made tacos for dinner. I loved taco night, especially when Mom served both the hard, crispy tacos and the soft flour ones. I liked to have one of each.

"One more week," said Lexi with a sigh. "I'll be glad when it's over. Win or lose."

"I know what you mean. But it's been so much work. What if neither of us earns enough money?"

Lexi shook her head. "One of us will win. One of us *has to.*"

I nodded. I wasn't sure what would be worse: having a cat, or having no pet at all.

Then I remembered I was talking to Lexi. Perfect, horrible Lexi. Having a cat would be way, way worse.

I eyed the hard taco tortillas on the plate between us. Lexi spied them, too. I reached for them. Lexi reached faster.

She grabbed all four.

"Hey, one at a time!" I complained.

"Says who, baby brother?" snorted Lexi.

"I'm not a baby!" I groused. "Mom!" She came over to the table carrying the lettuce and the tomatoes for the tacos. Not that I would ever put any vegetables in mine. I was purely a cheese and meat guy.

"Yes, Otto?" Mom said in a tired voice.

"Lexi took four taco shells," I whined, pointing. "She never eats four tacos."

"I'm hungry," she claimed. Mom threw her an I'm-not-in-the-mood look, and Lexi put one of the shells back on the serving plate. The shell cracked in half. "Whoops," Lexi said.

"She did that on purpose!" I hooted.

"No, I didn't," said Lexi.

"You're always ruining everything."

"No, I'm not."

"You're the worst sister in the world."

"You're the worst brother."

"We are not getting a cat," I growled.

"We are not getting a dog," she growled back.

"Otto! Lexi! Please!" yelled Mom. "Can't we just eat in peace?"

Lexi and I stared at each other. She opened her eyes wide, and I opened mine wider. I wasn't going to blink before she did. No way. But my eyes watered, especially my left one. It was getting increasingly hard to keep them open. I just had to concentrate a little more.

And I blinked.

Lexi smirked.

"So how is the challenge going?" asked Mom, picking up a flour tortilla. "Or shouldn't I ask?"

"Great," Lexi and I answered at the exact same time.

"My dog walking is breaking records for moneymaking," I added. "And I'm very responsible." I didn't mention all the problems I had.

"My sign painting is helping me explore my artistic side. It's important to be well-rounded. I should get extra points for that."

"Your butt is well-rounded," I said.

"You are so dead," Lexi spat, burrowing holes in my head with her eyes.

"Well, my dog walking is helping dog owners and dogs, so I should get double extra points for that," I said.

"I should get triple extra points because Otto is a loser," snapped Lexi.

"There are no such things as triple extra points," I yelled.

"There are no such things as extra points at all!" Lexi yelled back.

"If you two don't knock it off, this contest is over, got it?" Mom hollered.

So that shut us both up. I reached across the table and grabbed one of the hard shells from Lexi's plate, but I grabbed it too hard and the tortilla shell snapped into pieces.

"Nice job," Lexi chortled.

"I'm going to crush you like that taco shell," I muttered under my breath. Mom glared at me. "Just kidding!" I said with a smile.

Mom put down the soft taco she was in the process of folding. When she spoke, her tone was anything but friendly. "Is this about getting a dog, Otto? Or about beating your sister?"

"Isn't that the same thing?"

"I don't like how this is going," said Mom. "This should be healthy competition, not . . . *this*." She waved her hands while she said the last word.

"What's *this*?" I asked

"War," she said. "It's like war. And it isn't pretty."

"War isn't pretty," I grumbled.

"I wasn't kidding," said Mom. "If you two can't get along, no one is getting a pet. Understand?"

"I'm sorry, Lexi," I croaked, gritting my teeth.

"Me, too," said Lexi. I'm sure she meant it as little as I did. "Done!" she yelled. She somehow managed to eat two entire tacos while we were talking. "I need to go downtown and buy more art supplies. Can you drive me, Mom?"

"After I eat," Mom mumbled, picking up her newly created taco, but not looking particularly hungry. "I haven't even started my dinner yet."

"Well, I'll be waiting in the car." Lexi walked her empty plate to the dishwasher.

"I'm done, too," I muttered, wedging an entire taco into my mouth. I'm not sure if Mom understood a thing I said, since it sounded more like *I-o-woo*, but I wasn't going to let Lexi beat me at eating dinner fast, too. Besides, I had a dog walking appointment that night, and then I needed to do some homework, maybe. I didn't want to think about all the worksheets waiting for me in my backpack.

"Put your plate in the dishwasher," Mom ordered me. "And put away your jacket that's lying in the front hall." To both Lexi and me she yelled, "And I meant what I said! This is a family, not two countries!"

But Lexi was already out the door, and I was walking away from the table with my dirty plate.

Anyway, Mom was wrong. Lexi was the country of Stupid Kittenland. And I was the mighty United Dogs of America. And my country was counting on me.

When I returned home from dog walking that evening, homework waited for me. I sat at the kitchen table and opened my folder of schoolwork. What I really, *really* wanted to do, though, was sleep.

I had gotten some school assignments back that day. I hadn't done well, but at least I was passing my classes. I stared at all the red pen marks and the note from my teacher that read, "You can do better."

I wanted to write back, "But I can't do better or I'll never earn enough money and will have to live with a cat." I kept the schoolwork in my folder. I couldn't let Mom see it, at least not yet. I'd show her my grades after we had a dog. I knew Mom would fall in love with our new pet immediately and wouldn't get rid of it no matter how many Ds I got.

This was the stretch run. The final week. It was no time to slow down and start catching up on school. It was about making enough money. It was about beating Lexi.

If only there was a way to do homework and walk dogs at the same time. I tried that a few days ago, and my nose still hurt from when I walked into a wall while reading. So that wasn't going to work. Doing more than one thing at the same time is called multitasking. I needed to multitask.

I called Malcolm. "How are we doing on money?" I asked. I was a little nervous. We had talked at lunch. I had handed him his share of the earnings and told him how much money I had in my shoe box. He said he'd crunch some numbers to make sure we were on track. The deadline was looming.

There was silence on the other end.

"Hello?" I asked. "Anyone there?"

"Not good," he finally said. "We need to average about five dog walks a day to make it."

"Five a day?" I groaned. "Maybe if I skipped dinner. And school." And breathing.

"I have an idea," he muttered. "But. No. Never mind."

But you can't say *never mind* to someone, ever. Because the person always wants to hear what you're never-minding. "Out with it."

He cleared his throat. "No. It's a bad idea."

"There are no such things as bad ideas," I assured him.

"Of course there are. Bad ideas are a thing," he said. "Remember the firecracker and cauliflower incident?"

I would rather not have thought about that. "Fine. There are bad ideas. What's yours?"

He sighed. "It's a bad idea," he warned. "But . . . what if you walked more than one dog at once?"

My eyes grew big. My head shook up and down in agreement, although Malcolm couldn't see me. "That's multitasking!"

"Sort of," said Malcolm. "But it's a terrible idea, so forget I said it."

"It's a brilliant idea!" I yelled. "I can't believe I didn't think of it. Double-, triple-, and quadruple-book!" I boomed. "What do you call booking five things at a time?"

"Quintuple-booking?"

"Yes, that, too!" Real dog walkers don't walk just one at a time. They walk a group. "I want a quintuple-booked appointment first thing Monday after school!"

I'm pretty sure I heard Malcolm arch his eyebrows. "It's a lot harder walking more dogs. What if something goes wrong?"

"What could go wrong?"

"Really? I can think of about three hundred things without even trying. The dogs fight. They don't cooperate. You can't control them, you —"

"Fine, I get the idea," I said. "But this is my business. You work for me. Make the calls."

"You're being bossy again."

"Sorry. Just do it, okay?" I paused. "Please?"

"Fine. I'll book two dogs at once."

"Five dogs!" I insisted.

Malcolm sighed and said he'd start calling the next day. I hung up and opened my social studies textbook. I was supposed to read chapter eighteen, but I never made it past the second page in the chapter. I read it about eight times and I still had no idea what I was reading. I'm not sure how long

I was there, but when I woke up I was still in the kitchen, and my head was on the book and the sun was up. I was still on the second page.

At least it was something. I'd do the other eighteen pages of homework some other time. Soon.

From looking at the place, you wouldn't have known Lexi and I had spent the entire weekend cleaning Dad's apartment just two weeks ago. A pizza box sat on the kitchen table, three bags of garbage needed to be taken to the dumpster, and some dishes in the sink needed to be washed.

"Really, Dad?" I said. "You couldn't tidy up a little? And why does it always smell like peas in here?"

Dad sat on the couch, putting his feet up and lying back. "I've been busy. But now that you guys are here, I thought you'd like to help straighten up. And I like peas."

"No time to help, Dad," said Lexi. "I need to make signs." She had brought both her regular suitcase and a giant portfolio case filled with art supplies. She hurried into her bedroom to work.

"I hoped you could do some dusting . . . ," began Dad, but Lexi was gone. He looked straight at me.

"Sorry. I've got a dog walking appointment in twenty minutes," I explained, dragging my suitcase to my room.

"You guys can't help a little?" squeaked Dad in a small, desperate voice.

"Sorry," I said.

"Sorry!" hollered Lexi from her room.

"I could still change my mind!" yelled Dad. "Maybe I don't think a pet is a good idea!"

"Too late, Pops," I replied. "That ship has sailed."

Dad stood in the hallway outside our rooms. I didn't like to unpack when I visited, because that just meant I had to pack again in a day or two, so I threw my suitcase in the corner. "I've made some fun plans for us," said Dad. "I thought we could see a movie."

"Sorry. I'm too busy," I said.

Lexi yelled, "Me, too!"

"Lexi, we could go shopping!" shouted Dad.

"Sorry!" yelled Lexi.

"Otto, we could play soccer," he pleaded.

"Sorry," I said.

"We could play Sorry," said Dad, referring to his favorite board game.

"Sorry," I said, and then quickly muttered, "I mean, *no thanks*."

Dad stood in my doorway with a frown on his face.

He usually acted like he had to do some sort of father-kid bonding when we visited, since we only saw him every other week. But this was the home stretch. I didn't have time for parents.

I had responsibilities now. I couldn't play games.

But I had to admit that playing soccer and Sorry sounded fun.

"How's saving money going?" Dad asked as I hurried past him. "Good? You know I always wanted a dog myself."

"I know, Dad," I said, heading to the front door. He followed me.

"I thought we could go out to eat tonight," he said.

"I doubt I'll have time. Maybe we could just order in a pizza." I looked at his kitchen table and the pizza box sitting on top of it. "If you're not sick of pizza, that is."

"You know, I really need help cleaning out the storage closet downstairs," said Dad. "Really."

I started to answer, but Lexi appeared in the hallway before I responded. "I'll do it! How much does it pay?"

"It doesn't pay anything. I just need help," explained Dad.

"Oh. Then, no thanks," said Lexi, disappearing back in her room.

"Don't look at me," I said, holding my arms up after Dad turned to me and threw me an eager smile. "I'm booked." I walked out of the apartment.

"I shouldn't have to pay my own kids for quality father-child bonding time!" Dad cried after me. But I was already hurrying down the hall.

Although I did have one of his trash bags in my hand. I figured I could toss it in the dumpster on my way out. It was the least I could do.

When I arrived back at the apartment around dinnertime, Lexi was in her room and Dad was eating pizza by himself on the couch. I grabbed a slice and leaned back on the recliner next to him.

"How was dog walking?" asked Dad. "I'm impressed. Both you and Lexi are working really hard."

"If I don't work hard, we'll get a cat." I raised my voice so Lexi could hear me, "And we are not getting a cat!"

"We are not getting a dog!" she yelled back. Dad's apartment has thin walls.

"Growing up, your aunt Rosalyn wanted a cat," said Dad. "But I wanted a dog, just like you."

"What happened?" I asked between pizza bites. I needed to eat fast so I could make my final appointment, which was across town. Staying with Dad meant longer bike rides to get to my dog walking gigs. Half my time was spent traveling. I wished Dad lived closer to Mom's house.

"We couldn't agree, so we got neither. I ended up getting

a turtle, but I didn't know how to feed it and dumped the entire box of turtle food on its head, and it suffocated. I was only about five years old."

"It's much better having a dog," I agreed. "You probably couldn't buy enough dog food to dump on its head and kill it."

"Probably not."

"Any pizza left?" asked Lexi, entering the room. She snagged a slice and plunked down on the couch. I couldn't help noticing all the paint and glitter on her hands. There was some in her hair and on her nose, too.

"Done for the night?" asked Dad. "We could still catch a movie."

"Just taking a five-minute break," explained Lexi.

"I need to get going, too." I took a final slice for the road.

"Maybe next time," whimpered Dad, frowning.

"As long as Fluffernutter can come along," said Lexi with a giggle.

"We are so not getting a cat!" I yelled as I stepped into the hallway.

"We are so not getting a dog!" Lexi screamed back at me.

"You'll see!" I yelled, slamming the door. "This is war, you know!" But with the door closed, I'm not sure if she even heard that last part.

• • •

The next day, Dad didn't seem too disappointed we were leaving, although he had his game of Sorry sitting on the counter when we woke up. He put my glass of morning orange juice next to it and said things like, "I'm SORRY you can't stay," and, "SORRY you have to work so hard." I pretended I didn't understand what he was getting at.

When we got back to Mom's house, Lexi needed to run out and buy more art supplies. She goes through them faster than I go through candy the day after Halloween. We passed each other on the staircase.

"Dad seemed pretty bummed we're so busy," Lexi said.

I nodded. "Only a few days left, though. I can't believe you turned down the chance to go shopping!"

She smiled. "There's a first time for everything. Are you getting close to five hundred dollars?"

"Very close," I assured her. "Any minute now."

"Really?" Lexi laughed. "Any minute? You mean in two minutes you're going to have five hundred dollars?"

"Fine. Not any minute," I admitted. "But soon! Sooner than you!" I added, squinting my eyes. I hated when Lexi acted nice to me.

You shouldn't be nice to the enemy during war. It's just confusing. Lexi smiled and waved as she ran downstairs, but I glared at her the whole way. I had to be tough. Unforgiving. Vicious.

That's what war is all about.

I thought of horrible things I could do to her.

Cut off her hair.

Paint her face green.

Duct-tape her to the ceiling.

Steal her bed.

None of those ideas were good enough, though. After all, I owed Lexi a lifetime of payback for being annoyingly perfect all the time.

Winning this challenge and owning a dog would be the perfect revenge.

In her hurry to get supplies, Lexi left her bedroom door open. As I entered the second-floor hallway, I saw it. Just a crack. A streak of light shining from a window and onto the carpet by my feet. I hesitated in front of it. She was gone. Mom was downstairs. Somewhere in her room was a pile of money. How close was she? I kept imagining her riches, piles of gold coins raining down like from a waterfall.

I needed to know.

Just a peek.

Did I have a chance of winning this war?

So I crept noiselessly into her room. I knew she would kill me if she ever found out. Mom would probably let her. So I had to be careful. I wasn't going to do anything bad. Just count her money, that's all. See how close she was. And if she wasn't close, I could breathe a little easier and worry about my own money earning.

Her room was a world of sparkly glitter. There were a half-dozen signs in various states of creation: partly done, half done, mostly done, all done.

One of the boards said, GET YOUR FOOD AT SCHNOOD'S! but I couldn't bear to read the others. I seethed. First Mr. Schnood fired me, and then he hired the competition. I'd put him on the top of my revenge list, after Lexi. Maybe I'd go to his store and topple over another pyramid of cans.

That would show him.

I was pretty sure I knew where Lexi hid her money: in a jewelry box in the bottom drawer of her nightstand. She had showed me her cash supply when I was six years old. You should be careful what you show people. It can come back and haunt you later.

I pulled open the nightstand drawer. The jewelry box was sitting inside, with its painted pink princesses and unicorn stickers. I lifted the box, put it on her bed, and opened it.

Money. A big stack of it. And not just one-dollar bills, but fives and tens, and even a couple of twenties. I dumped it on the bed and had just started to count when I heard the front door close downstairs.

Lexi. She was back.

I recognized her footsteps immediately.

She must have forgotten something! But she would never forget me sneaking in her room. I threw the money back into the jewelry box, slammed it closed, and stuffed it back in her drawer. My heart pounded. As I turned to sprint out of the room, I saw a twenty-dollar bill on the bed. I didn't have time to put it back into the box, and I couldn't just leave it there as evidence, so I seized it. I stepped into the hall and stuffed the bill in my front pocket, just as Lexi walked up the final staircase step.

"Were you in my room?" she asked, narrowing her eyes.

"If I had been in your room, I'd be covered in grossness. So, no."

"You're already covered in grossness."

"That's from talking to you."

She rolled her eyes. I went down the stairs. From my pocket, the twenty-dollar bill stuck out. I stared at it.

I could use the money. I needed every dollar I could get my hands on.

This wasn't stealing, either. Not really. Lexi owed me for making my life miserable. She should pay me hundreds of dollars, and not just a small twenty. A lifetime of misery was worth lots more than this.

So why did I feel so guilty putting it in my shoe box later that night?

Mr. Hardaway frowned when he handed me the leash for Amber, his border collie. I stood on his porch with Mrs. Merryweather the poodle, Jim Jam the beagle, and Max the Jack Russell terrier. My first multiple-dog walking appointment. I wanted Malcolm to book five dogs at once, but he only managed to book four. He was probably right that I should start small. But eventually, I'd walk twenty, thirty dogs at the same time. I'd probably set world dog-walking records.

Maybe the old Otto couldn't have handled it. But for the new, improved, and mostly responsible Otto, this would be a snap.

Or not.

It didn't help that Mrs. Merryweather and Jim Jam were all antsy and barking, and Max wanted to run off and chase leaves. I read that dogs can sense whether you're calm. They smell it, like garlic. So I thought calm thoughts and shouted, "I'm calm! I'm calm!" in Jim Jam's ear, but it just made him bark more.

"Maybe we should forget it," stammered Mr. Hardaway, pulling Amber back inside.

"This will be great," I assured him. "Amber will make some friends. Everyone needs a friend." Amber seemed nervous, her head bowed. She hid behind her owner's leg as Jim Jam let loose a few loud *arf*s, and Mrs. Merryweather growled, and Max fought his leash. "Oh, their barks are worse than their bites," I said with a smile.

"They bite?" Mr. Hardaway cringed with concern.

"No, no!" I said, forcing a laugh. Mr. Hardaway didn't look convinced. That was okay, because I wasn't entirely sure, either. But it was too late to back out now. With a wave, I led the dogs, including Amber, down the sidewalk.

When walking a group of dogs, they are supposed to move in unison like an army platoon. That's what all the dogs do in online videos. But there must have been a secret to walking them that no one told me. Amber shuffled slowly forward. Jim Jam quickly rushed forward while barking at things. Max wanted to go somewhere other than the direction we walked. Mrs. Merryweather just wanted to poke the other three with her nose, mostly in their butts. They kept crisscrossing each other so their leashes got all wrapped together. I had to stop every few feet to untangle them all.

"Stop doing that, Jim Jam," I pleaded as he tried to jump on a jogger passing on the right. "No, this way!" I shouted to Max. "Just calm down, guys! I'm calm! Be calm!"

Max growled in response. Amber growled in return. Mrs. Merryweather poked Jim Jam with her nose.

We were halfway down the street when a biker rode by us. Jim Jam leapt at him. "Come on, guys. Can't we just settle down?" I howled. Jim Jam growled at the biker, jumping over Amber, who got down on her back and lay still. "What are you doing?" I screeched. Amber just lay there. I shook her to get her moving, but she growled at me. Then Max rolled onto his back. So I scratched his stomach, but that seemed to make Amber jealous, because she barked, and then Mrs. Merryweather started poking me with her nose. "Stop it!" I bawled. "Guys! We have to walk!"

Finally, they all stood up, and we made our way slowly down the sidewalk, Jim Jam and Max wanting to go in different directions from each other and from me. But we inched onward.

Jim Jam saw the squirrel first. Jim Jam barked, and then froze. The sudden stop made me stumble. The stumble made me let go of his leash. As I tumbled forward, I spied the squirrel standing under the tree. It hesitated for a moment. I was still stumbling. And then it took off.

Squirrels are fast. Jim Jam barked twice and took off after it, but not before smashing into Amber. Amber's and Max's leashes got tangled up, and Amber's sudden jerk yanked the leashes from my grasp. Mrs. Merryweather poked my butt as I was finally stopping my stumble, and then I tripped over her. I had the choice of either letting go of her leash or landing on my nose. I chose to save my nose. And just like that, all the leashes were flying behind the dogs, who were all off chasing the stupid squirrel.

"Help! Dogs on the loose!" I screamed, getting back on my feet and sprinting after them. I couldn't believe I had run-away dogs *again*! The squirrel had the lead, Jim Jam close behind, followed by Max, Mrs. Merryweather, Amber, and then me helplessly in last place.

"Jim Jam! Amber! Mrs. Merryweather! Guys!" I cried, running after them. "Be calm! Oh, come on!"

They scampered across four lawns, over bushes, and around trees. The squirrel was way ahead of them. I think it turned around and stuck out its tongue at one point, but I'm not entirely sure about that. It dove through a hole in a fence. The dogs were just small enough to get through, but I wasn't. I had to climb over it, and I fell and hurt my toe. We were in the backyard of someone's house. It was a large house with a big wooden deck and thick bushes crowded together, lining the side of the house.

The squirrel had apparently jumped into the bushes. The dogs followed and were stuck. They barked and bit and tried to get untangled. I limped up to them and grabbed their leashes, my head dripping sweat.

"Guys. Settle down. It's gone," I groaned, panting heavily. They didn't struggle as I pulled them out of the bush. But they were all covered in burs and yipping unhappily about it.

It took a long time to remove the burs. Max had over a dozen of them. The dogs were antsy but at least they didn't sprint away again.

By the time I got the dogs back to their homes, it was way late.

"What did you do to Amber?" cried Mr. Hardaway, removing a bur from her coat.

"Sorry. I missed that one," I said. "But I got the others out."

"Others?" Mr. Hardaway looked pretty mad. Amber looked pretty disheveled. Her coat was all ruffled, and dirt was caked on her nose. I couldn't look Mr. Hardaway in the eye. He knelt next to his dog, scratching behind her ear. "That's okay, Amber. You're home now," he soothed. "As for you." He pointed his finger at me. "I no longer need your services. You oughta *not* call Otto." He didn't even pay me.

The other dog owners weren't pleased, either. I guess I missed a bunch of burs, but in all fairness it's really hard to get them out when you're walking four dogs. Maybe Malcolm was right: multi-dog-walk-tasking *was* a bad idea.

You know it's funny about get-rich-quick schemes. They never seem to work out. I guess that's why there aren't that many people who get rich quick.

Despite the dog walking incident, I arrived at soccer practice on time that night, thanks to Malcolm's scheduling skills. He had blocked out a big chunk of time and written in thick, black marker: SOCCER PRACTICE. Coach should have been happy to see me, given me a slap on the back and told me he was delighted I could make it despite my hectic schedule. But Coach Drago wasn't the nice, slapping-on-the-back type. He was the growly, never happy, only-liked-to-say-bad-things-to-me type.

"Otto, pay attention!" he yelled. "Otto, what are you doing?!" he screamed. "Otto, run! Otto, kick! Otto, block! Otto, Otto, Otto!" I don't think he mentioned anyone else's name the entire practice.

But it's not easy playing soccer when your sister is getting rich making signs, you're really far from earning five hundred dollars, you're way behind in schoolwork, you have twenty dollars that's not really yours in a shoe box, and your soccer coach keeps blowing whistles in your ear.

Even worse, Malcolm had turned into the world's greatest soccer player. He was playing way over his head, and everyone's head — he kept heading balls into the net. I tried to head balls, too, but they kept hitting my nose. It does not feel good to have a ball constantly hitting your nose. That's why they are called headers, and not nosers.

It became obvious that Malcolm would be starting our first game of the season instead of me. During goal kicking practice he nailed every shot. I missed half. In dribbling drills he went around the cones flawlessly. I kept running into them. In juggling practice he was a whirlwind of ball motion, and mine kept bouncing randomly away. And then we played a scrimmage. Malcolm played with the starters and I played with the second string.

If only I hadn't taught him so many tricks before the season began!

"I'm not sure what I'm worse at, soccer or math," I complained to Malcolm as we took a water break. I took a big gulp of water from my water bottle. "I can't wait until this month is over."

"You know what Coach Drago always says?"

"'Otto, you're terrible'? 'Otto, pass the ball to Malcolm'?

'Otto, sit down'?" There were so many things he said that I couldn't pick just one.

"Other than that." Malcolm laughed. "He says to leave everything you have on the sidelines. If you play, play to win. And if you lose, at least you know you gave it your all. Have you given your pet challenge your all?"

"I think so," I said.

"That's all you can do."

But that wasn't good enough. There are no awards for trying hard, no dogs in your house for giving it your best. "Do I have a chance of earning five hundred dollars?" I asked, thinking of my shoe box filled with not nearly enough money.

Malcolm shrugged. "Unlikely. But you never know. And I do have an idea."

"Is it better than your last idea? I wish you hadn't insisted I walk four dogs at once."

"What?" said Malcolm, spitting out water from his water bottle. "I told you not to walk more than one dog. You didn't listen."

"That's not how I remember it," I grumbled.

"Do you want to hear my idea?" asked Malcolm. I sighed, and then I nodded. "So, my mom subscribes to magazines, right?"

"I could start a dog magazine!" I shouted. "Brilliant!"

Malcolm shook his head. "No, it's not. You cannot start a dog magazine. That's a horrible idea. But my mom pays for her magazine in advance, right? Last night she sent out a check for the next year of magazines. Why don't you offer dog walking subscriptions? Like a package. Pay now. Dog walk later."

"We can do that?" I was intrigued.

"Why not? Say, charge fifty bucks for a pack of ten dog walks. Normally, that would be sixty dollars, so it's a great deal for them. And you get your money now, when you need it."

I knew it would pay off to have a Mathlete champion helping me. "You're a genius." I could have hugged Malcolm right there and then, if it wouldn't have just been really weird.

"And I've been thinking," Malcolm said after taking a swig from his water bottle. "You don't have to pay me anymore. I want you to win."

My eyes must have bugged out. "Really? Are you sure you don't want your half of the money?"

"Twenty-five percent is not half. But yes. I'll work for free from here on out. Or at least until you get a dog."

"You're the best friend ever."

"I know. It's about time you recognized my extreme wonderfulness."

"It's hard to notice under your extreme ugliness."

"Cod-liver-oil spleen-vomiting rumpus worker."

"Gorilla-baiting eel hugger."

"Cockroach-infested motel-room rusted-tweezer lover."

But we were smiling the entire time.

"Water break's over, let's get going," yelled Coach Drago, clapping his hands.

I couldn't get the grin off my face the rest of practice, even after I tripped over an orange cone during our next soccer drill.

CHAPTER 25

When Mr. Colander instructed us to take out our pencils for the big math quiz, I almost raised my hand and asked, "What math quiz?" Today? Wasn't that next week? I thought the test wasn't until March 27.

Oh. Today was March 27.

I wrote my name on the top of the page, and it was downhill from there. It usually takes Mr. Colander a week to return our tests. That would be after we got a dog. Or a cat. No, a dog. So even if I missed every question, I'd still have a dog, and have someone to play with after I was grounded for the rest of my natural born life for flunking math.

Besides, this wasn't all my fault. Not really. Sure, I forgot about the test. Yes, I was doing lousy at school. But how was I supposed to concentrate when I saw signs from Lexi everywhere? When she smirked at me from across the dinner table?

When Malcolm was becoming the world's greatest soccer player?

But at least Malcolm was on my side, unlike my dreadful sister and her stupid signs. The school hallways were filled with them — I think everyone running for student body president hired her. There were dozens of glitter-gorged signs on every wall with expressions like, THINK BIG AND VOTE FOR SAM SPRIG! and GOOD GOLLY, VOTE MOLLY MYERSON! and PUNCH YOUR TICKET FOR ERICA RICKETT. It was enough to make you queasy and wish someone was running for office whose name didn't rhyme with anything.

I picked up a new dog for a walk that day. Barker was a Siberian husky. He had a thick white coat and the top of his head was black. He was all panting tongue and wagging tail. Barker also had the deepest ice-blue eyes you'd ever seen, eyes that just made you want to wrap your arms around him and give him a hug. Some dogs you want to roll around with, and others you want to run with, and others you want to stand back from and treat with respect and dignity. But with Barker, you wanted to hug him. He had a great smile, too, a smile that made you feel all warm inside, like you were wrapped in a warm, woolly blanket.

Hugging dogs. Now that I thought of it, those were probably the best kinds of dogs to have.

Barker was a medium-sized dog, but pretty thick. Huskies are sled dogs, so they're powerful and have a lot of stamina. This wasn't the sort of dog I was going to tire out.

"If you buy ten dog walking appointments now, they are only fifty dollars. That's a savings of twenty bucks!" I told Mrs. Mundsen, Barker's owner.

"Twenty dollars? I thought you charged six dollars for a walk. Isn't that a savings of ten dollars?"

"That's what I meant," I mumbled. Stupid math.

She only had twenty-five dollars in her wallet, but I told her that would be good for five more walks. She seemed hesitant until I assured her I was the most responsible dog walker on the planet, and did Barker have any eating problems, like with vanilla ice cream? Barker didn't.

I sold a package to Buttercup's owner, too. Although she said she would only pay forty dollars for ten walks, take it or leave it. I took it. Forty bucks is forty bucks. Just like that, I was back in the race. I was practically wealthy. I felt like the king of the world.

I put the money in my pocket, adding to an already sizable wad of cash. Ever since I'd snuck into Lexi's room, I had carried most of my money with me. If I accidentally took twenty dollars from her, she could do the same to me! So I didn't like leaving my money unguarded, even though my shoe box was way in the back of my closet behind a pair of shoes, and not just any shoes but the smelliest shoes I owned. Even I hated going near them.

Of course, if she took money from me, that would clearly be stealing. But I hadn't stolen from her — she practically owed me twenty dollars for a lifetime of being annoying. That twenty dollars was rightfully mine, right? Right?

Maybe if I thought it enough, I'd start believing it.

"Come on, Barker," I said. "Mush!" He bounded forward, but not before flashing me a smile. I bent down right in the middle of our walk and gave him a hug. Sometimes you just have to hug a dog.

With my dog walking subscriptions, the only thing that could stop me now was a horrible, four-letter word: *Lexi*. She had to be close to five hundred dollars. In fact, every time I came home I cringed, half expecting a cat to jump out at me. When I got home from dog walking, I cringed. When I woke up, I cringed.

"Why are you cringing so much?" Mom asked.

"No reason," I said, cringing.

I got home from walking Barker and I cringed, of course. But the house was still cat-less, so I uncringed.

As I went upstairs, I passed Lexi coming down. She has a way of crawling under my skin. Just looking at her brought a frown to my face.

"Only a few days left." She grinned. "Getting close?"

"Of course," I snarled. "Piece of cake."

"Cake? And we know what a good baker you are." She giggled. "Made any chocolate chip cookies lately?" I frowned. "Sorry," she said, and she sounded like she almost meant it.

But she couldn't fool me. Not for a nanosecond. "The only thing I'll be burning is you. When I smoke you in this pet battle."

Lexi rolled her eyes. "Maybe you can bake some cat cookies for Fluffernutter."

"We are not getting a cat," I yowled.

"We are not getting a dog," she hissed.

As she walked down the steps I paused in front of her room, fuming. I'd wipe that grin from her face. I'd show her that she wasn't better than me at everything.

I pushed open her door. A dozen posters sat on the floor, taunting me with their glitter and perfect lettering.

Lexi's nightstand stared at me, too, with beady, evil dresser eyes. It practically dared me to look inside the jewelry box again. I took a deep breath and thought of that twenty-dollar bill still sitting in my room.

I turned and left. I could beat her my way, fair and square. She'd see.

But as I walked to my room and put my hand on my doorknob to turn it, I saw a Post-it note stuck on the door. It had glitter poured on it and a single word: MEOW.

That did it. She couldn't mock me and get away with it. No more Mr. Nice Guy. I clomped to Lexi's room and threw open her door. I was sick of her. Sick, sick, sick. I picked up her signs, put them under my arm, and marched back out. I threw the boards on my bed and took out the scissors from my top desk drawer.

I'd show Little Miss Perfect. Let her try to win with all her posters cut into tiny pieces.

I grabbed the first poster in the pile, a green one that was almost finished. It said, PTA BAKE SALE, and below it but smaller, COOKIES AND CAKE, ALL FRESHLY BAKED! This would be the first victim.

Which seemed fitting. I bet the cookies only had one chocolate chip in them, if any.

I slowly closed the scissors, cutting the poster edge. I snipped some more. The slice grew longer, almost reaching the glitter.

And I stopped.

My hands trembled.

I dropped the scissors.

A bead of sweat dripped from my forehead and landed on one of the posters, smearing a letter.

I took a step back.

I couldn't do it.

I don't know what felt worse: cutting Lexi's sign or real-
izing I couldn't go through with the sabotage. I was aware of
how hard I was working. Lexi was working just as hard. I
knew all is fair in war. I knew it's kill or be killed. I knew war
is not for the squeamish.

But I thought about what Mom said. This wasn't war.
Not really. It was family.

Maybe winning wasn't everything. Maybe.

The board had a small slice in it, only about a few inches
long. I hoped Lexi wouldn't notice. I put the posters back into
her room. I think I put them back in the right places.

Chapter 26

Mr. "It takes me a week to grade tests" Colander handed back our math quizzes that very morning. Really? Just when things were starting to go right for me, too! I looked at my grade and felt like screaming. For joy. I didn't do great. A C− wasn't going to get high fives from Mom, but at least I wouldn't get a note home telling Mom I flunked. I actually yelped a little from excitement. I couldn't help myself.

"Yes, Otto?" said our teacher.

"Nothing."

"You yelped."

"Just happy."

"You got a C."

"A C minus. Isn't life wonderful?"

I felt so good I didn't even get upset staring at Lexi's wall of posters along the hallway when I left class. The student body elections would be next week, and the posters would all come down.

Next week life would be normal. Lexi's signs would be gone. I'd be a soccer star. I'd work extra hard to bring my grades back up. And I'd come home every day to an exciting, hug-ready dog.

"I got a C minus on my math test," I told Malcolm at lunch. "Fist bump!"

Malcolm made a potato chip, carrot stick, and peanut butter sandwich. That's when you open your bread and crumble your chips in it, and then add your carrot sticks. Malcolm said it made a sandwich that was crunchy and sweet and healthy all at the same time, but I just thought it was a waste of potato chips. "You know that a C minus is a horrible grade, right?"

"I think 'horrible' is a bit strong. 'Less than stellar,' I would say."

"No. It's horrible. I'd be grounded for a week if I got a C minus. But at least you're happy."

"It means I can still get a dog. I can still win." Malcolm finally returned my fist bump.

"Things are looking good," agreed Malcolm. "I was adding up your earnings. You've got some weird numbers, though. And you have about twenty dollars more than I thought you did. Where did that come from?"

"A generous tip," I mumbled, looking away, trying not to think of Lexi's hidden cash stash.

"Well, if you sell another subscription you could make it to five hundred dollars before the weekend. If not, you'll still squeak over. Just don't mess up."

"How could I possibly mess up?" I asked. "I'm the world's greatest dog walker."

Malcolm shook his head, and then took a bite of his sandwich. His crispy chomps sounded like someone walking on thin ice.

I chewed my cheese sandwich. Even I couldn't mess this up.

I was in an even better mood later when I walked Ruffy. His owner, Mrs. Singer, bought a subscription, and she didn't even argue about the price. Ruffy was a Lab with a beautiful, shiny black coat, so shiny it was like someone had sprayed it with cooking oil. You were proud to walk a dog like Ruffy, his nose up, his legs bounding up and down like you were in a parade.

Proud. Handsome. Those might have been the best kind of dogs, really.

Mrs. Singer told me that the last dog walker she hired let Ruffy run away, so I should be careful. I assured her she had nothing to fear with me, and that I would never let a dog loose (again). But I had nothing to worry about: Ruffy was incredibly obedient. He stood straight. He walked when I walked and stopped when I stopped. He even heeled when I told him to heel, and dogs hardly ever did that for me.

We entered the small downtown and passed a sign inside the window of the used bookstore, Ye Olde Town Curious Books. You'd think if you owned a book store you'd know how to spell the word *old* correctly. And what did *ye* mean? The sign in their window was one of Lexi's signs. No one else used so much glitter in so many awful colors as she did. I hated, hated, HATED to say it, but she did good work. There was a picture of a book made entirely of glitter, but you could practically feel the pages in your hand when you looked at it.

"What do you think, boy?" I asked. "Lexi has some talent, doesn't she? If only she wasn't so annoying. And a girl. And a cat lover. And lived in my house. And breathed my oxygen and got in the way and didn't like to watch any good TV shows. Other than that, she's not so bad, I suppose. Just don't tell her that, okay? Our secret?"

As we walked, we passed Mrs. McClusky unloading her weekly groceries again. She lifted what seemed like a really heavy bag, her back practically creaking. She looked like she needed some assistance.

"I can get that for you," I said. When you're on top of the world, it's easy to be generous.

"Thank you, young man," she said with obvious relief.

"Just hold this for a second." I handed her my leash and grabbed her bag. Or maybe I didn't hand her the leash. It happened so fast. One second I held a leash. The next second I heard, "Wait, young man, I don't have a good grip," while I was lifting the grocery bag. The second after that, I caught a glimpse of Ruffy tearing down the street, his leash dragging right behind him.

"Ruffy! Wait!" I cried.

"Oh, no!" exclaimed Mrs. McClusky. "What did I do?"

But she hadn't done anything. I had. I had been warned he liked to escape, too! I wanted to hit my head against the car door, but I was holding a giant bag of groceries so I couldn't, and I would probably dent the car. "Ruffy!" I cried, my stomach filling with panic. I bet he'd been planning an escape the whole time, pretending to be respectful and such.

Mrs. McClusky looked positively mortified.

"It wasn't your fault," I squeaked.

For a second I didn't know what to do. I couldn't exactly chase him holding a heavy bag of groceries. After a second of indecision, I put the bag down on the ground, but by then I didn't even see Ruffy anymore. "Where did he go?" I asked, my stomach tightening, my breath wheezing. "Ruffy!"

"I don't know," Mrs. McClusky said. "I lost sight of him."

I whirled this way and that. He couldn't have gone too

far. It had only been a few seconds. "Ruffy!" I cried. "Come back!" But if he could hear me, he wasn't answering.

If I used all my money, I could buy a new dog that looked just like Ruffy. Maybe. Probably not. But more important, what if something happened? He could be anywhere. He could be running in the street. He could have been picked up by dog-stealing hoodlums. "Ruffy! Ruffy!?"

How could I lose another dog? I was the most irresponsible dog walker ever. I didn't deserve to have my own dog. But right then and there I didn't care. I just wanted to find Ruffy. I just wanted him to be okay. I cupped my mouth and yelled as loud as I could. "Ruffy!"

Bark.

"Ruffy?"

Bark. Bark.

Ruffy came from behind the corner, marching slowly. Someone held his leash, walking him toward us. But not just someone.

"Lose something?" Lexi asked.

I ran up to them and gave Ruffy the biggest hug I could. I knew it was sappy, but my eyes watered. "I thought I lost you, boy!"

Lexi cleared her throat.

"Yes?" I growled, looking at her.

"I saw the dog running and I grabbed the leash. And then I heard your voice. Don't you have anything to say to me?"

"Like what?"

"Starts with a T and ends with a 'hank you.' As in, 'thank you for saving my butt.'" She smirked.

I gulped. I hated to say it. I truly, deeply wanted to say anything but this. But I said it anyway. "Yeah. Okay. Thanks."

"You're welcome." And then she threw me another smirk before walking away, and I wished I had said anything else. I wanted to scream after her: "Never mind my thank-you!"

But Ruffy was back and okay and that was the most important thing. I gave him another big hug.

This time I made sure Mrs. McClusky held the leash while I carried in her grocery bag. She insisted on giving me a ten-dollar bill even though I told her she didn't have to.

But it just goes to show you that there's such a thing as karma. You do nice things, and nice things happen back to you. And if you walk around smirking, then karma bites you in the head.

I'd win this war because I deserved to win. Because karma was on my side. Unless karma knew about that twenty dollars I accidentally took from Lexi. No, that twenty dollars she owed me.

Maybe.

At breakfast, Mom announced that there would be a meeting on Saturday. A pet meeting. That's when we would let her know if we had saved enough money. That's when we would discover what sort of house we would be living in — would we have a lousy, catnip-infested, stuck-up, stinking cat house, or a friendly, outgoing, best-friend-boasting dog one?

"Are you guys getting close to earning enough money?" Mom asked. "The month is almost over."

"Very close!" I said, my mouth full of oatmeal.

"Exceptionally close!" said Lexi, nearly coughing up a cornflake.

"Really, exceptionally, brilliantly close!" I shouted in a garbled croak. Some oatmeal dribbled down my lip.

Lexi didn't even try to top me.

But this time I meant it. I had counted my money when I woke up. I'd make it to five hundred dollars with a day to spare, unless something went horribly wrong.

And what could possibly go horribly wrong? I thought. After all, karma was on my side.

"We'll see on Saturday," said Mom.

I tried to read Lexi's face. Was she confident? Nervous? Scared? I couldn't tell. Lexi's expression didn't change. She might have smirked, I wasn't sure. If she did smirk, it was a very, very small one.

"Otto!" yelled Mom. "Your shoes don't belong in the kitchen!"

I walked Barker again. It was part of a subscription, which means I had already been paid for walking him. It sort of felt like walking a dog for free. But a subscription is a commitment. It's a responsibility. And I was nothing if not responsible.

Besides, I really liked walking Barker. Every time he looked up at me, his tongue wagging and his eyes filled with joy, I wanted to melt right into the pavement. I would have walked him for free.

But walking him for money was even better.

I pretended Barker was my dog, ambling along the sidewalk. My dog, barking at strangers. My dog, sniffing invisible creatures and standing at attention when threatened by a flower.

My dog would be the sort of dog that wouldn't run away, even if I dropped the leash, because it loved me so much.

My dog wouldn't shed. It would growl at crooks and sisters.

My dog would be smart and do tricks.

Most of all, my dog would love me more than anything in the entire world.

I couldn't imagine anything better. It would have made this month — the grades, the soccer, the guilt — all worth it.

"Hey, wanna play soccer?" It was Eric and Kyle from the soccer team, approaching and waving from down the block. They kicked a soccer ball back and forth between them. "We're heading to the park," said Eric.

"I shouldn't," I said, glancing at Barker.

"Oh, come on," said Eric. "We'll play for ten minutes. Twenty minutes tops."

"Well, I . . ."

"We'll meet you there." They ran ahead.

It was tempting. It was. I could tie Barker to a branch while I played. This time I'd tie the leash exceptionally well. Barker wouldn't mind. I needed the practice. I imagined Coach Drago applauding as I kicked in the perfect goal. "That's the way!" he'd scream. "Otto's back!"

"It was nothing," I'd answer, blushing. "I've just finally had some time to practice."

Playing soccer wouldn't be goofing off. It would be the responsible thing to do. I wasn't just practicing for myself; I was practicing for the team. I couldn't let them down!

I didn't pay attention to where we were walking. I was too busy kicking an imaginary soccer ball through the net and dreaming of Coach Drago's excited clapping. That's why I didn't notice the broken bottle on the sidewalk. I should have been more alert. I should have been looking out for Barker, who was distracted by a biker and didn't see it, either. His shrill bark snapped me out of my daydream.

Immediately I knew something was wrong. Barker stood on three legs, whimpering. Blood dripped from the pad of his lifted paw. Shattered glass covered the sidewalk. Who would leave a broken bottle like that?

Barker looked at me with those large eyes of his, but they weren't smiling eyes. They were helpless, desperate ones. There's nothing you can do when a dog looks at you like that, other than wish you were the one bleeding from stepping on glass. I would have traded places with him in a nanosecond.

I knelt down to look at Barker's paw. There was a glass shard sticking out, and I started breathing hard. My heart pounded. A couple of weeks ago I would have panicked.

Dogs can feel your nervousness. I had to be calm, but not for me. Barker would be calm if I was calm. I took a deep breath. I slowed my heart.

"It's okay, boy." I held his paw in one hand and rubbed his neck with the other. "We'll get help." I slowly pulled the piece of glass out. Barker whined.

I knew of a small vet clinic at the edge of downtown. Just a few blocks away. I couldn't expect Barker to walk, though, and he was too big to carry all that way. "Stay here, boy!" I said to Barker. I dropped his leash, which felt strange, but he wasn't going anywhere. Not with that foot.

"Help!" I yelled, flailing my arms to catch the attention of a small and sporty green convertible driving past. The car screeched to a stop. The door opened. The driver stepped out.

"Thank you, mister," I said before I even noticed who it was. The man wore an apron with blood splattered on it. He was tall and frowning. It was Mr. Schnood.

"Oh. It's you," he grumbled.

I ignored his groan. "The dog. He's been hurt. Please, Mr. Schnood. Can you drive us to the vet? It's only a few blocks away." He paused. He looked at me, and then at Barker. And then at his car.

I expected him to drive away. He didn't look very happy to see me. But then he nodded. "Okay. Let's go."

As it turned out, Mr. Schnood wasn't so bad. He helped me carry Barker to the car and put him on the passenger seat. I climbed into the very tiny back. I could only fit on the seat by sitting sideways.

"We should call your mother," Mr. Schnood said, taking out his cell phone.

"No. She's out of town," I blurted out. I didn't want Mom to hear about this. Or Lexi. She would just say I was being irresponsible and that's why the dog got hurt.

No, I needed to prove I wasn't mostly responsible. But that I was *really* responsible.

"Who can I call?"

"No one. I'm fine. Really. Just hurry."

When we pulled up to the animal clinic, Mr. Schnood helped me carry Barker into the building. There were four or five chairs in the waiting room, but they were people chairs, which was kind of crummy for the animals. They were the ones who were sick. There was a bulletin board with pictures of dogs that owners must have sent in (I doubt the dogs dropped them off). I recognized a couple from my Dog Party Debacle. The place smelled like cleanser. For some reason I thought it would smell like animals.

"Thanks, Mr. Schnood. You can go now. We'll be okay."

Mr. Schnood sat down. "I'll wait. You might need a ride

back home." He grabbed a dog magazine from the end table and opened it.

As I said, Mr. Schnood turned out to be pretty decent when you weren't knocking over his cans or putting grocery bags in the wrong car.

A man in a white lab coat was eating a fast-food hamburger behind the counter. He had a scraggly white beard that reminded me of a sheepdog. I didn't know who he was until he put down his burger and walked around the counter and held out his hand. It had mustard on it. "Sorry. I'm eating a late lunch. I'm Dr. Radis. What happened?" He wiped his mustard fingers on his sleeve. Still, I didn't bother to shake it.

"His name is Barker. He stepped on some glass," I said. "Is he going to be okay?"

"We'll take good care of him," the doctor assured me. He looked more closely at the paw. "It doesn't look so bad. More of a puncture. Let's clean it up." Dr. Radis lifted Barker and carried him. "Your dad should come, too," he said, nodding to Mr. Schnood.

"Oh. Um, he's okay right there," I blurted, avoiding the whole that's-not-my-dad-and-this-isn't-my-dog conversation. I didn't know whether the doctor would treat Barker if he knew he wasn't my pet. "He faints at the sight of blood. And he doesn't speak English."

"Then why is he reading a magazine in English?"

"He likes to pretend."

The doctor sighed but nodded. We went through some doors and into an examination room. It was sort of like a human doctor's room, although the exam table was small, steel, and on the floor. Dr. Radis put Barker on the table, and it lifted when he pressed a button. After washing his hands, the doctor listened to Barker's heart and pushed on his belly and chest.

"It's his foot," I pointed out.

"Just checking," said the doctor.

Finally, he treated the paw. "It's okay, Barker," I said, petting his side. I fought my nerves so that I stayed calm and my heart didn't race. "You'll be fine, boy." Barker gave my hand a lick and then closed his eyes as the doctor cleaned out the cut and wrapped it in a few layers of bandages. The final bandage was bright green, which was way cooler than a plain old white bandage if you ask me.

When the doctor finished, Barker panted and looked up at me with those deep ice-blue eyes. You'd have melted if you saw them, believe me.

If this is what being really responsible felt like, then I guess I liked being really responsible.

"He will heal right up in two or three days," said Dr. Radis. "The bandages should be changed every morning. I'll give you a couple days' worth of pain medication."

"I don't think I need pain medication," I said.

"It's for the dog."

That made sense.

We went back to the reception area. "How much do I owe you?" I asked, fishing out the wad of bills I kept in my pocket.

"It was eighty dollars. But he took care of it," said the nurse, gesturing to Mr. Schnood.

Mr. Schnood looked up from his magazine. "Is he okay?" I nodded. "Ready to go?" I nodded again.

Barker wore a little bootie on his paw, so he could walk, but slowly. It obviously hurt, but he didn't complain. That was the sort of stand-up dog Barker was.

"I want to pay you back," I said to Mr. Schnood as we approached his car. This was *my* responsibility.

"It's on me. I'm sorry I had to fire you. We'll call us even now." He leaned over to me and whispered, "Mrs. Printz is a pain in the rear, if you ask me."

I got into the backseat, but I couldn't let him pay. I was the one who was responsible. Me.

I removed eighty dollars from my pocket. "Here," I said, thrusting it forward as Mr. Schnood backed out of the parking lot.

He shooed me away with his hand. "It's on me."

"I insist," I said again, putting the money on the front seat. "My mom will pay me back." Which of course was a lie, but Mr. Schnood shrugged and took the cash. "Thanks for driving," I added.

"No, thank *you*. That magazine I was reading gave me an idea for a new display. A pyramid of dog food bags." He paused. "Bags, not cans," he added warily. After driving in silence for a bit he said, "I guess you can come back to the store. Not to work," he quickly added. "But to shop. You're not so bad, kid."

"You're not so bad, either, I guess," I added awkwardly.

Mrs. Mundsen didn't take the news of her dog's injury as badly as I thought she might. I explained what happened and gave her the instructions for taking care of Barker. I didn't think she was going to hire me again, but she didn't yell or threaten to sue me.

That night at home, I lay in bed with my shoe box next to me. I counted my money, twice. There was no way I could earn enough money for a dog now. I had even missed all the rest of my appointments that day because of the vet visit. I called my customers to explain. They were understanding, except for Mrs. Linkletter, who complained that she never should have bought a subscription. I told her I would throw in an extra dog walking day and that made her happier.

But I knew I'd already lost the challenge, and there was nothing I could do to make enough money to win, short of selling all my clothes and Mom's computer. And selling Mom's computer wouldn't get me a dog, it would just get me grounded for the rest of my natural born life, my unnatural life, and probably three or four other lives as well.

Yet I felt calm, just like they say you're supposed to feel when you walk dogs. Even though I was going to lose the challenge. Even though I would be living with a cat, I had taken responsibility. Being responsible means accepting what happens even when things don't go right. Being responsible means not blaming someone else, either. Even though I really, really wanted to blame everything on Lexi.

CHAPTER 28

It was pretty late that night when I sat at the kitchen table, my math worksheets spread in front of me.

Lexi sat at the table, too, doing homework. She had as tall a pile of sheets as I did. I hadn't seen her a lot the last few days, since she was always making signs or buying art stuff.

She looked up and saw me staring at her. "A lot of homework?" she asked, pointing to my stack.

"Maybe," I replied, waiting for her sneer. "You?"

"Too much," she said with a sigh.

"Yeah, right," I scoffed. There was no such thing as too much homework for Little Miss Perfect. The more the better.

"I've been working so hard that I'm way behind in school."

I waved at her stack. "Please. You can probably get through that in like ten minutes."

"I wish. It's going to take days to catch up. I just hope Mom doesn't see my grades before tomorrow."

"Get a few As instead of A pluses?"

"No," she groaned. "I've been making signs. Tutoring. Doing everything but studying. I don't get good grades by blinking, you know."

"You don't?" Blinking was one of my theories about why she did so well.

"No. I work really hard because I have to, not because I want to. If you spent as much time on your homework as I did, you'd get straight As, too. I just know that school's important."

I stared at her, my mouth open. Sure, I saw Lexi study. But I thought that was because she liked it. I never really thought Lexi actually studied because she needed to.

"It's called being responsible. Not that you would know anything about that," she grunted.

"I know more than you think," I mumbled. "Especially now. So, when are you getting Fluffernutter?"

"What makes you think we're getting a cat?"

"Because I lost. I don't have enough money. We'll have a cat and every day you can gloat."

"I don't have enough money, either," she admitted.

"B-but I see your signs everywhere," I stammered. "You tutored like everyone in school." I didn't mention the stack of bills I spied in her jewelry box the other day. Or the twenty dollars I had taken.

"I gave a lot of those signs away for free. I figured it was good advertising. People would see my signs and want one. But when I sold them, I didn't get paid enough, and art supplies cost a fortune. Do you know how expensive glitter is? But everyone kept wanting more and more glitter and I couldn't say no. I didn't make that much from tutoring, either. Kids just don't have a lot of money. And half my friends aren't even talking to me because they said I was mean. I don't know. I just got frustrated when they didn't know the answers. I guess I'd make a poor teacher."

"Well, you make a poor sister, so I suppose that's fitting," I said, smiling.

"I make a better sister than you do a brother."

I nodded my head. "You're probably right." I sighed. "I thought you never had problems."

"I wish! I can convince Mom to do stuff. But try to present charts to your friends and they just think you're weird." She threw me a half very-non-smirky smile. "I haven't been too nice to you lately. Sorry. I guess I just got carried away with our war."

I nodded. "Tell me about it."

"I can't even count money right. I somehow lost twenty dollars," she groaned. "How do you lose twenty dollars?"

I squirmed in my seat a little. "Yeah, that's strange." I looked down at the table. "Then I guess we're not getting a pet."

"I guess not. A shame, huh? After all that work, too."

She was right. We were both doing poorly in school. We had both sacrificed a lot. Not having any pet seemed unfair. I mean, I knew cats were stupid and I hated them. But maybe a cat was better than nothing. What's the point of having a war if both sides lose?

But I guess in some wars that's how it works. There aren't winners in wars, not really. Just one side that does less awful than the other one.

"How much did you earn?" I asked.

"More than four hundred dollars. I was really close. You?"

"Less than that. Hold on."

I went up to my room and removed my shoe box from behind my smelly shoes, only gagging once. I took out the money. I could have done a lot with that cash. I could have bought that two-hundred-dollar pair of sneakers I really wanted. Or that ultraviolent but ultracool video game I read about. I knew I was handing victory to the enemy. But somehow it felt okay. It felt right.

Maybe Mom was right. There are more important things to spend money on than sneakers and games.

Besides, twenty dollars of it was Lexi's. I had stolen it. There wasn't any other way to put it.

But first, I counted out the money I owed Mom for her bowls, and her toner, and her pencils, and the other odds and ends I had used, taken, or broken. But there was still a lot of money left for Lexi and her cat. Our cat.

"Here," I said, handing her my money after I came back downstairs. "It seems silly for us both to lose."

"Really?" Her eyes grew wider and wider as she looked at the money. "But this is way too much."

I shrugged. "Well, not all of it is mine. Remember that twenty dollars you lost? I took it. I don't know why I did. I just got carried away, too. I wanted to see how close you were and it just sort of happened. I wanted to win so badly."

Lexi nodded. "I looked for your money once. I wanted to know how close you were, too. But I couldn't find your loot. And I didn't want to look in your closet. Your sneakers really smell."

"That was the idea."

Lexi picked up my stack of bills. "I guess this makes up for your stealing."

"I hope so." The way Lexi looked at me, all grateful and stuff, it almost reminded me of Barker and his wide-open thankful and trusting eyes. I almost had the urge to hug Lexi, but I'm glad that feeling faded away quickly.

"Maybe you're not the world's worst brother," she said.

"Thanks. I guess you're not the world's worst sister. Maybe just second-worst. There must be someone who keeps her brother locked in a cage and force-feeds him peas. That sister would be worse. Maybe."

Lexi smiled and grabbed my homework. "Let's see if I can help you a little here. I bet we'll get through this in no time. After all, I'm an expert tutor."

"But what about your homework?" I asked.

"I'll get to it. Come over here. A big sister is supposed to help her baby brother, right?"

"I'm not a baby."

"I know, I know."

"So," said Mom, intertwining her fingers as we sat around the kitchen table. "Today's the day." She smiled at Lexi and me. "How did it go?"

"Great," I said. "Easy."

"Really?" said Mom, surprised. "The contest is over, but if we get a pet, it will still be a lot of work. For both of you."

"We've talked about it," I said. "I'm going to still walk dogs, but I'm going to cut down quite a bit."

"And I'm going to tutor again," said Lexi. "But a lot fewer students."

"So I guess that means we're getting a pet," said Mom. "Otto?"

I shook my head. "Not a dog. I didn't make it."

Mom arched her eyebrow. "Really? You worked so hard, too. And you were being responsible — don't think I didn't notice."

I handed her an envelope filled with bills. "This is the money I owe you. For the toner. And the bowls and stuff."

"I thought we were missing some bowls."

"Sorry," I mumbled. "I guess I wasn't always responsible. But I tried. And we'll have to talk about my grades, too."

"I guess we will," she said in a not-very-pleased voice. But then she turned to my sister. "Lexi? How much money did you earn?"

Lexi put a large wad of money on the kitchen table, a wide grin on her face. She smiled, but there was nothing sneaky or smug about it. It was just a happy smile. "Five hundred dollars," she said. "For Fluffernutter."

"Congratulations, Lexi," I said, and I meant it. I didn't tell Mom about our conversation last night. I didn't tell her that Lexi had fallen short, too, but we had succeeded together. This was Lexi's moment. I was actually happy for her, sort of, kind of.

I know she beats me at most things, but maybe that's because she works harder at it. I can't hold that against her, at least not totally.

It would be nice to have an animal in the house. And who knows? Maybe Fluffernutter would hate Lexi and love me. I wondered if I could make that happen. Keep some milk hidden in my room. Have a drawer filled with secret cat toys. Pipe supersonic noises into Lexi's room that are too high for the human ear to hear but that a cat could, so it would stay away.

This wasn't about getting a cat. This was war.

No, strike that. I was done with wars, for now. "Can we get it today?" said Lexi. "There's a house a few blocks away giving away kittens. I just happened to see a posting on a website on your computer this morning. There was a picture, too! They are so cute: golden yellow with streaks of brown. I know just the one I want. There's one kitten that looks just like a Fluffernutter."

I admit it. The kitten was cute. She didn't have claws yet, so when she swatted your fingers it felt like velvet cloth rubbing against them. When you held her in your hands she purred softly, her stomach vibrating. I knew she would grow up to be a standoffish, not-very-cute adult cat, a yucky, good-for-nothing flea ball, but for now she wasn't so bad.

And I hated to admit this, too — but she sort of looked like a Fluffernutter. I wouldn't have named her that, of course. And I would never tell Lexi the kitten looked like a Fluffernutter. But the name seemed to fit. And Lexi called her Fluffy for short, which wasn't as awful.

I'd have plenty of time to play with her since Mom grounded me for two weeks because of my grades, except for school, dog walking, and soccer. Frankly, I feared worse.

Fluffy bounded across the carpet and landed in my lap, where I gently scratched behind her ears.

"She doesn't dislike you," said Lexi. I think there was a tinge of jealousy there. After all, Fluffy had bounded into my lap and not Lexi's. "But I'm sure she will grow to hate you as much as I do."

"She can never hate you as much as I hate you," I shot back.

"Lame brain," said Lexi.

"Cobweb cranium."

"Dumb skull."

"Cerebellum-challenged amoeba-minded hollow head." But we both smiled after I said it.

And you know what? It turns out I'm better at insults than Lexi. Who knew?

Lexi lifted the kitten from my lap and held her in her arms. I watched her stroke Fluffy. I liked her more than I thought I would, but she was still no dog. Everyone knows dog people are clever, friendly, good-looking, funny, and overall fantastically wonderful, and cat people are not. Just because I tolerated Fluffy didn't mean I had turned into a cat lover overnight.

Maybe in a year or two, I could convince Mom that two pets were okay. A cat *and* a dog.

The sound of barking interrupted my thoughts. A joyful, loud bark from outside. At first, it made me a little sad, as if

I were being teased, but the barking was getting louder, and closer. It came from behind the front door, and the doorbell rang.

When I answered it, there was Dad, holding a leash. Standing next to him, tongue and tail wagging, was a beautiful light-brown golden retriever. At first I thought it was Alfalfa! But this was just a puppy, and when I looked into his dark eyes, I recognized him.

"Thumper!" I said.

"Dad? What's going on?" asked Lexi. She and Mom came into the hall behind me.

"You know I always wanted a dog as a kid," said Dad. "And all this talk of dogs made me realize I still wanted one. Mom called me yesterday and told me that Lexi won the challenge, and so I decided that maybe I could be the dog owner of the family. His name is Horseradish."

"His name is Thumper, Dad," I said.

Dad shrugged. "One of the great things about having your own dog is you get to name him. I've always liked the name Horseradish."

I questioned Dad's choice of names, but I couldn't question his choice of dogs. I bent down and Horseradish ran over to me, leaping on my knees and licking my face. I grabbed him and rolled on the floor, rubbing him as his tail wagged and his tongue raced up and down on my cheek.

Horseradish was the rolling-around type of dog. He was the licking type of dog. He was the loving and happy type of dog. Most important, he was my very own dog (almost). And really, those are the best kinds of dogs of all.

"Can I . . . ," I started to say.

"You can come over and play with him whenever you want," said Dad, stepping into the front hall and closing the door behind him. "You, too, Lexi."

Lexi still held Fluffy, and she came closer, slowly. Fluffy didn't seem scared, she just stared at Horseradish with her curious black eyes. Horseradish barked happily. When Lexi sat down closer, Horseradish nudged Fluffy playfully with his nose.

"I think he likes her," said Dad.

"I'm sure they'll be best friends." Mom laughed. I bet this was all her idea.

"Can I take him for a walk?" I asked.

"Of course. You are the expert." Dad smiled.

"Is it okay, Mom?" I asked. "I'm still grounded."

"Go ahead," she said with a wide grin.

I ran to the mudroom and grabbed my shoes and jacket, where I had hung them the day before. "Come on, boy." I beamed, grabbing the leash from Dad. "I know a whole bunch of good trails we can take. And, Dad?"

"Yeah?"

"We need to talk about his name."

Fluffy meowed good-bye, or at least meowed, and I was off with Horseradish. "But Horseradish is still a much better name than Fluffernutter," I added, shouting over my shoulder as I stepped outside.

I had soccer practice that night. I showed up on time and Coach Drago hardly even screamed at me at all. We played a scrimmage and I scored two goals, the last one after I faked one way, kicked the other, and left my defender so confused he tripped, leaving me a wide-open shot. Malcolm scored three goals. And you know what? We both played on the first team, Malcolm on the left, and me on the right. But I bet we'd be really good, no matter who started. After all, it takes a team to win a game. Just like it takes a team to win a war.

ACKNOWLEDGMENTS

Growing up, my dad was allergic to dogs and cats, so we had fish. Fish are not the most exciting pets — very few of them play fetch. So I need to give a loud shout-out (bark-out?) to the following dog lovers, owners, and experts for sharing their cat wisdom and dog anecdotes since I had none from my youth: Dr. Eve Cheung, Karen Oppenheim, Stephanie Shulman, Elisa Yuter, and most especially Dr. Kiran Singh and the generous staff of the VCA Hawthorn Animal Hospital. I'd like to also thank my kennel-full of expert critiquers (and outstanding authors) Suzanne Slade, Barb Rosenstock, Michele Weber Hurwitz, Sherry Randle, Juli Caveny, Susan Stephenson, and Carole Vaughn.

This book would not exist if it weren't for the remarkable Jody Corbett, editor and inspirer extraordinaire, and her group at Scholastic. Also, if it weren't for the efforts of Joanna Volpe, Danielle Barthel, and the staff of New Leaf Literary.

I need to also thank my long-dead pet turtle and fish — particularly Fred and Ginger Fish — whose stories of demise in this book are, unfortunately for them, completely true. Lastly, thank you to my sister, Deena, or at least the twelve-year-old version of her, for inspiring numerous conversations and confrontations in this book. We may have argued often, but we both know I was always right and I was Mom and Dad's favorite.

ABOUT THE AUTHOR

Allan Woodrow grew up in Michigan, always wanting to be an author. But his teachers told him to write about what he knew, and he discovered he didn't know very much. It turns out he didn't know very much for quite a long time. Allan isn't sure he really knows anything more now than he did in third grade, but he got tired of waiting and decided to start writing anyway. He is the author of *The Pet War*, the Zachary Ruthless series, and other books for young readers written under secret names.

Allan currently lives near Chicago with his family and two goldfish. The goldfish are vicious. For more about Allan and his books, visit his website at www.allanwoodrow.com.